A MALICE

Love

2

A NOVEL BY

BIANCA

© 2017

Published by Royalty Publishing House

www.royaltypublishinghouse.com

CHAPTER 1

Malice

*C*an you imagine standing in the doorway, in front of the woman who has paid you between two and three thousand dollars to rock her fucking world, twice a week, and sometimes three, and the woman who makes your heart smile just at the sight of her? I'm telling you to imagine that shit, but this is what's happening to me right now. I'm standing here looking at Kambridge Lewis, the source of my true happiness over the last month or so, and the woman, Tracey Lewis, who has been getting the bottom knocked out of her pussy by me, over the same amount of time.

How the fuck did I get caught up in this? Lewis is a common damn last name. How the fuck did I manage to snag the two that live in the same household? I thought to myself. Maybe I should have asked Kam what's her mom's name instead of just... oh my God!

Tracey and I were just staring at each other in disbelief. I'm sure that she was thinking the same damn thing that I was thinking. If I didn't know anything else, I knew that yesterday was our last time fucking. I was going to miss them few thousand bucks she was throwing my way, but there was no way I could continue fucking her knowing how I felt about Kambridge Lewis. I looked my little woman up and down as she stood by her mom's side. She had on one of my silk button-down shirts, wearing it as a dress, that stopped right under her thighs. She had on a pair of open-toe heels, showing off a fresh white set of pedicured toes. I bit the inside of my cheek because sucking her toes had briefly run across my mind. I shouldn't be thinking about sex, but my little woman is so fucking sexy to me. She had her natural hair in a big twist out, and her makeup was flawless as usual.

"Hey, Mom! This is Malice, or Phoenix. I think he prefers Malice most times. Malice, this is my mom, Tracey Lewis." Kam introduced us and laid her head on her mom's shoulder.

Tracey's eyes never left mine. Even with Kam and her mom both staring at me, I could see no fucking resemblance. I saw the pictures of her dad, and she didn't look like his ass either.

My arm was shaking as I held it out to shake her mom's hand. Tracey didn't even try to hide her disdain for me, keeping her arm flat by her side. I put my sweaty palm back at my side when I realized that she wasn't going to shake it.

"Kam, can you get my briefcase out my trunk, please?" her mom asked just above a whisper.

"Mom, you never bring your briefcase⊠" she started.

"DO LIKE I ASKED!" she yelled, making Kam jump a little, and that instantly pissed me off.

The minute Kam was out of earshot, Tracey spoke.

"Are you out of your fucking mind? Showing up to my house like this. Using my daughter to stalk me," she spoke through gritted teeth.

"Bitch, please. Not even in your fucking nightmares would I stalk you. Kam and I been cool for a little minute now," I replied coolly.

"I got your bitch! You weren't saying that last night when you were in my guts. Does my daughter know you a fucking male escort?"

"Does your daughter know that her mom pays for sex although she is a married woman?" I countered, cocking my head to the side.

"Fuck you, Malice, or *Phoenix*."

"Cool. The rest of your appointments are canceled anyway. I couldn't hurt my little woman like that," I said.

"Wait, no..." she started, and I scrunched my face up at what I thought she was about to say.

"Mom, I didn't see it," Kam said from behind me.

She walked up behind me, and I put my arm around her neck. I rubbed my nose through her hair, and it smelled so good. While I was rubbing my nose through her hair, I kept my eyes on her mom, who was now staring at me with a look of jealousy on her face.

"Okay, maybe I misplaced it. Thank you for looking for me," she said with a half-smile.

"Come on in, babe. Let me show you around the house," Kam offered.

We stepped in the house, passed her mom, and she grabbed me on my ass. I turned around to look at her, and she had a grin on her face. This bitch had to think I was just playing, but I wasn't in the slightest. I ain't going to fuck with her like that no more. She got shit to lose, just like I got shit to lose. Her daughter being one of them.

Inside of Kam's house was so dope. The house was filled with all type of art that I would never spend money on. The house appeared to be so inviting, but one wouldn't believe what goes on behind these doors. We started upstairs, and she showed me all the bedrooms, including hers. Her bedroom smelled just like her, and I wanted to throw her in the bed and make love to her.

We made it back downstairs, and my stomach rumbled at the smell of the food.

"This is my dad's office. When the door is closed, that means he doesn't want to be bothered," Kam said.

The second we walked away, the door opened and her dad appeared.

"Malice, this is my dad, Judge Kason Lewis," she introduced us.

Neither one of us held our hands out to shake it. Him and I stood eye level and glared at each other. Pure hatred was in both of our eyes. Every time I blinked, I saw Kam crying and screaming for help as he beat her like she was an animal. Once Kam realized that there was not about to be any speaking between us, she pulled me away from him. Walking away, I could feel him glaring a hole in my back, and I squeezed her ass because I knew he was watching.

I followed her down in the dark basement, and she turned on the lights. I ain't never seen a basement this neat before. Her violin was in the middle of the floor on the stand, and in the corner, was the pottery station.

"This is where I play the violin. I try to practice new music at least twice a week," she said.

I nodded my head, and walked over to the small door that had several locks on it.

"What's in here?" I asked her.

"Good question. I've never been in there. Dad keeps it locked, and there is only one set of keys to get the door opened."

My common sense came alive, and I couldn't help but think that this was where he kept my dad's gold, but if her dad was as smart as he said he was, he would not have kept the gold in his house.

"Cool," I said making a mental note of the door.

"Come on, dinner may be ready now," she said.

She started up the stairs, and I came up behind her, running my hand up the shirt, grabbing her little petite ass. She jumped at my cold hands on her skin, and let out a little moan.

"Why you stealing out my closet? Don't act like I don't know my shit when I see it," I laughed.

"First, when they made your shirt, they didn't stop making them. Tom Ford didn't say, 'let me make Phoenix's shirt and don't make any more,'" she laughed.

She walked up a couple more steps, and I grabbed her by her thighs, stopping her. I pushed her over, and I took a knee. I raised the shirt over her ass, and she had on a lace thong. I swear since I bust her wide open, her pussy lips have gotten even fatter. Her pussy lips were swallowing her thong. I started licking and sucking on her exposed pussy, and her knees started buckling, which turned me on even more.

Ripping her thong off, I ran my tongue up and down her ass. I spread her cheeks open and pushed my tongue in her ass. That brought her down to her knees. I could tell that she was trying to hold in her moans. Lightly plucking her clit made her cum quick as hell, and I stuck my tongue inside of her, making sure I don't miss a damn drop. After she came, she fell flat against the stairs. I bit both of her ass cheeks, before I got up and helped her to her feet. She turned around to face me, and I stared into her hooded eyes.

"You are such a freak! Why did you do that? This is my parents' house," she whispered like we weren't the only people in this basement.

"You liked it," I smirked. "Now, when I get you out of here, it's going to be hell to pay because my dick is hard as hell, and I can't get this shit down right now."

She grinned and tried to snatch her thong out of my hand, but I stuffed it in my pocket. It was ripped anyway, so there was nothing that she could do with it. She came down a step, making us eye level. She placed her big juicy ass lips on mine, and we started tongue wrestling. I ran my hand up her shirt, and her pussy was wet as hell. It was getting wetter the more we kissed.

The door opened, scaring the shit out of her.

"What are you two down here doing? I been calling for you two for the last ten minutes. Dinner is ready," her mom snapped while standing at the top of the stairs with her arms folded across her chest.

"Um, I was showing him my violin," Kam said, and started up the stairs.

I followed behind her, winking at her mom while walking past her. I could tell that she was hating. Kam told me that she was going upstairs to clean herself up, while she led me into the dining room where everyone was. I popped a piece of gum in my mouth so I wouldn't be smelling like Kam when I talked to these people. I took one of the empty chairs between Kade and Kalena, right across from their dad, who was looking at me like he had a problem with me.

Moments later, Kam came and took a seat next to me. I kissed her on her cheek, and I don't know who I made the maddest, Tracey or her father. I was truly enjoying this.

"So, Mr. Bailey, what is it that you do for a living?" her dad asked me.

"I'm in school for business, and I cut hair on the side. A little bit of this, and a little bit of that. I've been saving my money up so I can purchase a building to open my own shop. I would like to say that my little woman inspired me," I said and looked at Kam who was smiling her little ass off.

"How did you two meet, and when? Are you two dating? Having sex?" Tracey asked.

"Mom!" Kam screeched. "What is your problem? You have never..."

"I got this, mama," I assured Kam, by placing my hand on her thigh to stop it from shaking. "Mrs. Lewis, Kam and I met at her store a month or so ago when she made my jerseys with my logo on it. I was so captivated by her beauty that I had to get to know her. My little woman and I are taking things slow, but whenever she decides that she wants to take this a step further, then we will start dating...exclusively. It's her world, and I am truly just living in it. I'm obsessed with everything about her. Her drive to be great, her mindset, her smile, the way she handles the obstacles that have been thrown her way. I can't imagine my life without her friendship," I said.

I looked at Kam, and she wore a look of shock on her face. Nothing I said was a lie, but I definitely said that to fuck with her parents.

"Who are your parents? What do they do for a living?" her mom asked.

"My parents are Paxton and Angela Bailey. My dad owns his own taxi company, and my mom is a housewife."

"Paxton as in Korupt?" Tracey asked, and her eyes grew wide. Then she looked at her husband and put her head down.

I nodded my head, and her facial expression changed quickly. Tracey got up and came back a few minutes later with a cart full of trays. These folks in here were really living like the Huxtables, but had more secrets than the kids on the popular show *Riverdale*. I hated that Kam had to live like this.

We were eating in silence, and I only made conversations with Kam and her siblings. Her mom and dad kept eying me, making me smile every time. Kalena got up and whispered in Kam's ear, and then left out the room. She got up, pulling her chair and the one Kalena was sitting in, to the front of the dining room. Moments later, Kalena came back with Kam's violin, and gave it to her.

"Phoenix, I wanted my sister to perform for you. She's good on this thing. This is something that I could never get down with, but I do have some vocals, though," Kalena said, looking at me with a big smile on her face.

I smiled at her. Looking at her family members, Kam really don't look like anybody in this family. I wonder if she was adopted or something. She leaned over and whispered in Kam's ear, and she looked insulted.

"Girl, don't you ever downplay my skills like that. Of course I can play that song. You know she is the Queen," Kam replied.

Kam started playing the violin, and seconds later, Kalena joined in and started singing. It was Beyoncé's song that she sung for Jay-Z. I think it's called Die with You or Die for You or something like that. I knew the song because Kam had it on repeat for hours a few days ago.

Listening to the words of the song and looking at Kam play her violin, made my eyes water because I knew that at some point, this thing that we were doing was going to come to an end. A very nasty end. The secrets that I was holding in, no relationship or friendship could survive it. Kam's eyes were closed as she was playing her violin, and I could tell that she was playing with everything in her heart. The serious faces she was making tore my fucking heart up, because I knew that in her heart, those words were meant for me. I looked at the floor because I just couldn't stand to look at her and listen to her sister sing. My head popped up when Kam joined in with her sister and started singing.

"Cause darling I wake up just to sleep with you. I open my eyes so I can see with you, and I live so I can die with you," she sang.

The lone tear was sliding down her eye, as she was singing and playing the violin at the same time. I ain't even know that you could play the violin and sing at the same time. When they finished the song, Kade and I were the only ones clapping for her. Her mother and father sat on the other side of the table looking stupid. I wish I could have smacked the stupid look off both of their faces. She smiled at me, and I smirked back at her. I couldn't even smile the way I wanted to because I knew that I was going to break her big heart one day.

After dinner was over, Kam and I were standing outside by my car. I opened the door and leaned against it, pulling Kam towards me. She rested her arms around my waist, and had her head against my chest, fucking up another one of my shirts with that makeup shit.

"How was it? I knew my dad was going to act crazy, but I ain't expect my mom to start acting the way she did. That was truly weird to me," she said.

"Girl, I ain't worried about your parents. I had a good time, and your violin and singing skills are bomb as fuck, shorty. You gon' have to sing for me personally one day," I said.

"What are you about to do now? You want me to come to your house?" She looked up at me with her bright eyes.

"Nah. I'm about to go kick it with my bro for a minute. I'm going to call you later. Is that okay with you, little woman?"

She nodded her head, and she placed her lips on mine. We tongue wrestled for five minutes. She tried to unzip my pants, but I caught her wrist and told her no. We kissed one more time, and I watched her walk in the house.

∞

"If I had just let that bitch in the hood make my shit, I wouldn't have been in this predicament, bro! What are the fucking odds that the two Lewis women that I'm fucking are some kin to each other. I never even put two and two together. Well, Tracey never discussed her husband, and I didn't ask. Kam never said her mom's name. Mane, I can't talk to either one of them anymore." I expressed my feelings to Mayhem while pacing in front of him.

"That do sound like a fucked up situation. You can just leave shorty's mama alone, and then do your thang with your *lil' woman*," he said, mocking the way I called Kam my little woman.

"Dude, the minute I pulled out of their driveway, her mom was texting me, bro. She talking about she don't want to stop our appointments because Kam would never find out. What type of shit is that family on, man? That could sound like a plan, but whatever is done in the dark will come to the light. Fam, you know that. You think I could go to the grave without letting Kam know that I fucked her mama?"

"So, you telling me that you are just going to stop talking to Kam cold turkey? You going to let that girl text you back to back to back to back, and you just not respond? You were her first; she may just go crazy on you. She may be quiet, but never underestimate a scorned woman. The best thing for you to do is just … shit, stop fucking with her mama and keep fucking with Kam. It's not like her mom is going to tell her daughter that she is paying her nigga for sex, and ruin her marriage to her father, and her relationship to her daughter."

"You're right, man. This shit is wild as fuck. I'm going to figure out something," I assured him.

I went in my room and got in the bed. Looking at the ceiling, I knew that there was only one thing that there was to do. I had to just leave Kam alone. I wouldn't fuck with her mom either, but I didn't think I could just look in Kam's face knowing that I used to beat down her mom.

Cat Jenson

My heart was truly broken after Malice left my house. I hadn't seen him since, and he barely answered any of my calls. I swear I called him damn near a hundred times a day, but he only picked up a couple of times. When he did pick up the phone, I'd be begging him to come give me some dick, and he'd say no. After he'd tell me no, I'd end up going crazy on his ass, and he'd tell me that's why I couldn't get no dick now. When he'd tell me that, I'd hang up on his ass, and break my phone. I'm seriously on my fifth phone since he walked out of my house, after choking me out. He is acting like I told the bitch about us. I could have, but I didn't. I've been texting him and telling him that I want some dick, but he doesn't reply at all.

He's truly been stressing me out, and I need like three glasses of wine just to make myself go to sleep. Every free moment I get, I'm following him around and checking out his tracker to see where he's been. He barely rides his motorcycle now, and it's frustrating because now I have to guess where he is, but I still have his calendar synced to my phone.

After pouring me a glass of wine, I pulled the pictures out of my bag that I had been taking of Malice and his clients. I would follow him to the hotel, and take pictures of him walking in and leaving. His clients were very secretive, so you would never see them together unless they walked together to their cars after leaving the hotel. A normal person wouldn't put two and two together of an older white lady and a young black gentleman walking out the door of a hotel together. So, I had a few pictures of him with his clients—only a few though. A couple of weeks ago, I saw him walking out the hotel with a black lady, which was surprising because Malice has never had a black client. I couldn't be mad at that, because she was very beautiful.

I looked at my phone, to look at his calendar, and matched up the name with the client, and got a Tracey Lewis. I put her name into the search engine, and the first thing that popped up was who she was married to. My eyes got big as hell when I realized who she was. This lady was Kam's mom. I chuckled to myself because this was going to be good. When I looked at his calendar before, I saw the name Tracey but that's all it was. So I never would have put two and two together. If Malice is as cool as he says they are, I'm sure that he knows about this shit.

I smirked at this newfound information, before I picked up the phone to call Malice to gloat about the information I knew. Surprisingly, he picked up on the first ring.

"What do you want, Cat?" he growled into the phone.

"Don't be so mean to me, Malice. I want you to come over here! NOW! You better be over here in less than twenty minutes, or I'm going to call over to the damn t-shirt place and let your little whore know what her beloved *friend* does to make money," I snapped and hung up the phone.

I didn't even give him time to respond. I knew I could get him to respond when I mentioned that bitch. I grabbed the pictures of him and his clients and stuffed them back in the folder and in my briefcase. I slid it under the bed, and waited patiently for him to come barreling through the door. I didn't change the locks, so he could still use his key.

Twenty minutes later, Malice walked slowly into the house. He had on all black, and he looked stressed out. He hadn't had a haircut, and he hadn't lined up his facial hair or none of that. His eyes were bloodshot red and half closed, which meant he was high. He looked delicious in his black jeans, black boots, and plain white t-shirt. I bit the inside of my bottom lip as I surveyed him from head to toe.

"What you want, Cat?" he sighed.

"So, you doing mother and daughter now, huh? You having a threesome with a mother and a daughter now, huh? Are they both paying you?"

"Cat… I don't have time for this. Wait, how you know that anyway?"

"I have my ways."

He shrugged before he replied, "Look, I don't talk to either one of them anymore, so do whatever you want to do with that information." He turned to walk away.

"Look, don't you miss this?" I asked, and then dropped my robe to show my lingerie set I had on.

He turned around, looked at me, but he shook his head and headed for the door again. Like a maniac, I ran behind him and started hitting him in his back, while screaming my head off.

"STOP ACTING LIKE YOU DON'T GIVE A FUCK ABOUT ME, MALICE!"

He shook me off him and opened the door to leave. I started crying again. I hated what this man was doing to me. I didn't even feel this strongly about my damn husband.

"Oh, I'm giving you back the motorcycle as well. Don't want you to try and hold that over my head," he said nonchalantly.

"Fuck you, Phoenix. Keep that fucking bike," I snapped, and slammed the door in his face.

I slid down the door to the floor and cried my eyes out for the rest of the night.

∞

"You been acting funny ever since your little girlfriend broke up with you. I thought that's what you were waiting on, so we could be together," Holly, one of my students said to my other student, Connor, who didn't look as good as he normally looked.

These kids had been studying for the bar exam for the last six months, and they took it last week and failed. All of them. Miserably. I was so pissed when I got the emails from them.

"Leave me the fuck alone, Holly. Can't you see I really don't want to be bothered right now? I ain't never tell you I wanted Kam to break up with me. *You* wanted Kam to break up with me," Connor snapped.

"Forget you and that black ass girl. Your parents don't even like her anyway," Holly said, pushing his head.

I was tuned in, but I was even more tuned in now because I heard Kam's name, and Holly called her black. This couldn't be a coincidence because I knew that Kam went to the same school as they did.

"Connor…Holly… everything okay?" I asked, hoping I could get some information out of them.

"Yeah, I'm fine. It's him that has the problem. His black girlfriend broke up with him, and now he's been acting like a girl, and she's the reason he failed the bar exam," Holly responded.

"What was your excuse?" Connor turned his head and asked her before he turned back to me. She just rolled her eyes at him. He continued. "I don't know. I love her, but… I don't know. We had been together for a long time. It's just that I let my colleagues get in my head about the way that she looks. I mean, Kambridge is so beautiful, regardless of her skin color. I mean, that's what attracted me to her from the beginning. She is my best friend, and I treated her like crap because of what my parents were saying, my friends were saying, and now I lost her forever. The only thing is, and what I can't seem to wrap my mind around is…who the hell would have told her that I was in the restaurant with this girl?" he said.

I remembered seeing Holly and Connor in the restaurant that night I followed Kam and Malice to that restaurant, but I didn't think anything of it. If they saw me in the restaurant, then Kam had to see them in the restaurant as well. I smirked to myself because I had so much ammunition that could ruin Malice and that bitch he thought he was going to give his heart to. I didn't care that he said they didn't talk anymore. I didn't believe that shit for one second. I ended the conversation with my students and started helping their crazy asses on the bar exam that they would be taking again in sixty days.

Kambridge

*T*here was no song, words, person, pastor, or even God that could help me understand the way that I am feeling right now. I hadn't seen or spoken to Phoenix in two whole weeks. He wouldn't pick up the phone for me, and I had even gone by his house, but no one answered the door for me. This man had me doing things that I had once criticized other women for doing. He never took me to the other side of town, so I didn't even know where he cut hair, and I felt like an idiot ass bitch. I lost respect for Malice because I thought that if he didn't want to fuck with me anymore, he would have at least had the decency to tell me to my face. This nigga damn near thirty, and couldn't face a twenty-two-year-old face to face.

I was having a slow day, so I had Shelly sitting with me in my store. She kept trying to cheer me up, but nothing she said or did could cheer me up.

"Do you think he took another girl on the trip that I purchased for him?" I asked Shelly.

"Girl, no. I'm sure there must be an explanation for this disappearance. Do you think that he is dead or in jail?"

"I have checked every morgue in the city, and I have searched every obituary site, and there is nothing there. I called every jail, and they don't have a Phoenix Bailey. I feel like such a bitch for even caring right now," I expressed.

"Girl, you let that dude beat your walls down. You know you are going to care. You love the guy, and personally, I don't see how your ass fell in love in a month anyways. Soft ass. You wasn't supposed to fall in love," she laughed.

"Girl, whatever. That man's sex is immaculate, but all jokes aside, he is everything that I never knew I needed in a man. I just don't get why he would shut me out. I mean, I get that my dad was an asshole, but that's not a reason for him to treat me like shit. It's truly frustrating," I sighed.

She was getting ready to say something, but she rolled her eyes toward the door.

"Don't look now, but your boy just pulled up," Shelly said.

My heart started beating because I thought that it was Malice, but it was Connor's bitch ass. I ain't talked to his ass since I told him to go be with Holly. A part of me still loved him because I gave him a lot of my life, but I felt like he had been lying the whole time about Holly, making me look stupid. Connor walked in the store, and I took in his wardrobe. He had on a blue Polo t-shirt, khaki shorts, paired with some khaki Sperry's. He even had on a dad hat turned to the back. I shook my head at how sexy he was, but he was such a bitch to me now.

"Kambridge, is there somewhere we can go and talk?" he asked.

"Connor, I've had this shop for a year now. You know we can go in the back and talk," I said.

He unhooked the latch on the door and walked through the curtain to the back. I told Shelly to watch the front while I walked to the back to talk to Connor. He was leaning against the table, looking at me with a look of sadness in his eyes.

"Kam, I want to apologize to you, but Holly truly means nothing to me. I promise."

"Connor, if she meant nothing to you, then you wouldn't have gone on the date to begin with. Please miss me with the bullshit," I said, holding my hand up in his face.

"Kam, I swear I love you so much, and I don't want to lose you. You have to believe me," he pleaded.

"I don't have to believe shit, Connor! I'm done with you, but I do have a question though. How many times have you took Holly on a date? How many times have y'all had sex? I know y'all have before. I'm not crazy."

I asked that because Holly had been making my life a living hell ever since Connor and I had been together. There was no way that one chick would have just kept messing with me, if something had never happened between them. I'm truly not even sure I wanted to know, but I asked anyway. I had to choose my words wisely because I didn't want him to know that I was with another guy, and that I was the one who saw him in the restaurant with her.

"Um, I'm not going to lie. I only had sex with her twice. Twice. That's it, and that's been years ago. I let her give me head a few times, but that's it. I haven't had any type of contact with her in over a year," he confessed.

"Connor, how the fuck you keep saying *'that's it'* but then keep adding shit to what you did with that white bitch? Please get out! I don't want to hear anything else," I snapped.

"You have to give me another chance. I'll get on my knees and beg you," he said, getting on his knees, wrapping his arms around my waist.

"Nah," I said, trying to pry his arms from around me.

He kept his arms around me, and after I didn't say anything else, he stood up, crossing his arms across his chest. We glared at each other momentarily before he started stroking his barely-there beard.

"You know what I can't seem to wrap my finger around, Kambridge," he said.

I put my hands on my hips and cocked my head to the side, waiting for him to say something stupid.

"Funny how you saw me at the restaurant, but who were you there with? No way you went to that restaurant by yourself. I know that bitch out there wasn't there to tell you that she saw me."

"Watch your fucking mouth, white boy!" Shelly yelled from the front, making me chuckle. "You don't know where I was. Your daddy probably took me. Mind your business. Not my fault you sloppy."

"Stay out of this, Shelby Jean!" I replied.

His face started turning red. I knew that he was mad because Shelly said something about his daddy, and I was trying my hardest not to double over in laughter. It took everything in me to keep a straight face.

"First, I never told you that I saw you at the restaurant. Try that lawyer shit on someone else, not me. Just know I know that you were there and that we are over." I shrugged.

"Please, Kam! You were there because I'm not stupid."

"You stupid if you think I'm about to sit here and argue with you about it. I said what I said, and now it's time for you to leave."

He rubbed his hand down my face, and then squeezed my chin as hard as he could. I swear it was like I could hear the bone in my chin crack. His face turned red, and he had a look of the devil in his eyes.

He sighed. "Kam, darling, I'm going to give you time to be mad, but you and I will never be over. You are *my* piece of dark chocolate, and I will not lose you. Now, I told you that what Holly and I had was over, and it's true. So, take that how you want to take it, but we will be back together soon. I don't want the other side of me to come out," he spoke and then smiled.

When he let my chin go, I was scared out of my mind, but I didn't want to show any fear. That smile plastered on his face let me know that he was clearly crazy, and there probably was a side of Connor that I had never seen before.

"I'll die before I get back with you, Connor Wiles," I spoke through gritted teeth.

He smirked before he leaned down and whispered in my ear, "Let's not speak things into existence, shall we."

After he said that, he smacked me on my ass and then walked out the back, leaving me standing there staring at the wall. I looked at the camera and watched him walk out the door. My heart started beating fast as hell because Connor had never threatened me like that before. I was seriously shaking. I walked out the back, and Shelly was sitting there on the computer.

"You have an online order that just came throu … Kam are you okay?"

"Yeah, I think so. I'm not sure if Connor just threatened to kill me or not."

"Bitch, please! Connor is such a bitch, and wouldn't bust a grape in Welch's backyard. He's just trying to scare you into getting back with him. He ain't never been without you this long and he's just reacting. I can promise you that," she assured me.

"I've never seen him like that before. He was literally smiling while telling me that he would kill me."

"Kambridge, fuck him. Come get this order off this computer. If you don't feel safe, get you a pocket knife and some mace."

I nodded my head and pulled my phone out to text Kade. I ain't want to get him alarmed or anything, but I just wanted to let him know.

Me: Hey, you busy?

Kade: Never too busy for you, what's up?

Me: If I tell you this, please don't overreact. I just want to give you a heads up.

Kade: Kambridge! Don't fucking play with me. What the fuck is going on? I already got a feeling I'm about to react.

See, I ain't want Kade to do this, so I just didn't text him back. He called and called, but I didn't pick up the phone. Ignoring Kade didn't last long because thirty minutes later, I heard tires screeching outside, and I looked up to see Kade's car damn near in my store.

"Damn, girl, why Kade pulling up like he the FEDS?" Shelly asked.

He yanked the door open and stomped into the store. I could tell that he already had an attitude.

"What the hell type of games are you playing, Kambridge Leeann Lewis?" Kade asked.

"Look, I ain't want you to get mad so that's why I stopped texting you. I don't want to tell you because I know that you going to say something to him, and I don't want you to do that."

"Girl, you ain't got to tell me not to say nothing to Malice, because he was at the restaurant with us looking sick. So whatever he did⊠"

"Nah, it's not about him. It's Connor. I think he threatened to kill me, but I don't know."

He tried to walk away from me, but I grabbed his arm. He kept trying to snatch away from me, but I kept the tightest grip on him.

"Kambridge, let me go, for real. I'm not going to hurt him, but when I'm finished with him, he's going to wish he was dead," he snapped.

"No! No! Please! I don't think he was serious. He was just mad that I'm not getting back with him. Please, no. If he says something else to me, I promise I will let you fuck him up," I begged.

"Alright, Kam. First and last time I'm letting this shit slide. You better tell me if he says anything else to you, and I mean that shit," he said and walked out the door.

I silently cursed myself for telling Kade because I knew that he would probably say something to him. I prayed that he didn't and just let it go.

"Girl, Kade is going to beat Connor's ass. I don't even know why you told him," Shelly laughed. "If he swung on a Bailey, Kade will beat the fuck out of Connor, and I hope I am there to see it."

"Anyways, I'm about to go back here and work on this online order. Can you please lock the door when you leave? Leave the keys in the door, and leave out through the back."

She nodded her head, and I went in the back to start working on the shirts. I put my Beats on my head and started working hard. Even working today couldn't keep my mind off of Phoenix's big head ass. I couldn't believe he'd been treating me like I was just the regular hoes that he had been dealing with. All that *I want to make love to you* bullshit was just that—bullshit. I'm just glad that I had never told his ass how I really felt about him. Pushing him to the back of my mind, I got the shirts done in two hours. I printed out the shipping labels, put them on the boxes, and then set myself a reminder to go to the post office in the morning. After cleaning up the room, I gathered all the trash and took it out the back to throw the garbage away. When I walked back in the room, I rolled my eyes at the sight of that six-foot red ass man leaning against my table. He held my keys in his hands, which let me know that Shelly's ass didn't lock the door good. I silently cursed her ass out.

"Oh, hellll no! Get out, Phoenix," I said to him while pointing to the door.

"Kam, please let me explain." He set my keys on the table next to him, got up, and moved toward me, but I backed up.

"No, I don't want to hear what lie you are going to come up with. I know my dad is unbearable, but you could have at least kept it a hundred with me and let me know that you were done fucking with me instead of leaving me high and dry," I snapped. "Do not come close to me if you are not walking by me to leave."

He crept toward me with his hand out like he was reaching for me.

"I'm not about to leave, Kambridge. I just need to explain to you⌷"

I swung at him, and he dodged my lick, grabbing my fist, and twisting my arm behind my back, making me turn around. He grabbed my other arm and placed that one behind my back as well. The only thing that was stopping my back from touching his chest was the fact that he had my arms behind my back. I couldn't move at all, and I swear it felt like if I did, my shoulder would pop out of place.

"Owww, let me go! My arms hurt," I cried.

"Kambridge, I know you mad, but do not put your hands on me. I would never put my hands on you," he growled in my ear. "If I let you go and you hit me, I'mma hit you back."

He let me go, and I turned around and stared at him. My eyes were full of water, and one blink made the water pour from my eyes. I looked into his eyes, and his were red as well.

"Why didn't you just tell me that you didn't want to fuck with me anymore? I would have respected you more if you did that shit. You got me combing obituaries and jail lists, looking for your name. You got me going by your house and knocking on your door like a stupid ass obsessed bitch. I hate you, Phoenix. Please get out. I don't ever want to see you again," I cried.

"Come here, Kam," he whispered.

I turned my head and looked at the wall, ignoring him. He walked towards me, and my body did not move back like my brain told it to. He wrapped his arms around me, but I didn't reciprocate the action. He kissed my forehead.

"I have to be honest with you, Kambridge," he whispered and backed away from me.

I wasn't sure what he was about to say, but I braced myself for whatever stupid excuse he may let leave his lips. I looked at the floor because I didn't want to look into his face.

"Look at me, lil' woman!" he whispered, and I met his eyes.

"I love you, a'ight, and I don't need to. I'm not good enough for you just yet. I have way too much going on, and I know I can't give you all the love that you deserve, so I bounced on you. The last two weeks, without your touch, has been miserable for me. You see how I'm looking, but I just couldn't waste another day without telling you how I felt. I'm sorry. Do you forgive me?"

"So, you dip on me because you love me? What type of shit is that? What does that even mean? You can't love me the way I deserve, but I thought you said that we were just going to chill until we were ready to make things official. Apparently, you are not ready to make things official, and I would have understood that. I thought we had that understanding from the beginning though, Phoenix, I don't understand."

"Kambridge, I don't understand myself at times, and I am truly sorry. How can I make it up to you? I'll do anything," he pleaded.

I shrugged because I didn't know what he could do to make it up to me.

"Why are men so afraid of love? You literally ran away from it. Men would rather be miserable than be with the woman they love."

"Men love really hard, Kambridge. Really … hard. Let me explain something to you. Love makes men vulnerable, and in this world, there is barely room for men to feel vulnerable. Men fear rejection, and had I told you that I love you, and you said that you didn't love me back, that would make feel like shit. If you tell me that you don't love me, I will probably never tell a girl that I love her first again. You make so happy, Kam, and with happiness comes a chance for pain. I think that I would much rather be miserable than to potentially face a heartbreak that I'm just truly not ready for. I don't think I'm mature enough for a heartbreak that you could cause. Mane, if you break my heart, I would probably cry like a baby or something, I ain't gon' lie. Last thing, I'm insecure. Very insecure. I know that it doesn't seem like it, but I am. You're twenty-two and very accomplished. I'm nowhere near where I want to be in life, and I feel like you might leave me for another man who's more accomplished. So, there you have it. That's why I left. I was scared. So, if you ask me if I rather be miserable than experience an emotion that I have never felt before, hell yeah! I can deal with being miserable, but a heartbreak? Nah," he said.

After he said what he said, he brushed past me. I grabbed his wrist, stopping him from taking a step further. He turned around to face me, and I stood on my tiptoes, and placed my lips on his. We swapped spit, momentarily, before I pulled away. I turned the lights off in the room and went outside to my car.

"So are you coming over, mama?" he asked as he held my door open for me.

I nodded my head, and he walked over to his car. The whole time I was following him to his house, I kept thinking about what he said to me. We both loved each other, but I just can't see my dad letting me be with him in peace. We parked in his yard and went in his house, kicking my shoes off at the door like we always do. I honestly couldn't wait to get him to his room.

"Come here," he said and pulled me in the bathroom.

He ran the towel under the water for a few moments and then started cleaning my face off. The whole time he was cleaning my face, we were making eye contact, and he was biting his big ass bottom lip.

"You look so much better now, lil' woman," he whispered. "Now, come here."

He pulled me in his room and closed the door. I sat on his bed while he walked over to his stereo. He turned the music up a little, and the surround sound made it sound like we were in a movie theatre. He hooked his phone up to the stereo as well and turned on some fire crackling sounds, so it sounded like we were sitting in front of a fireplace. He turned around and was slowly bobbing his head to Xscape's song "Softest Place on Earth."

Baby you can be the first, inside the softest place on earth, he mouthed and then pointed at his heart. He motioned for me to stand up and placed kisses along my jawline while unbuttoning the dress that I had on. We locked lips the minute my dress hit my feet. He slowly laid me down on the bed, staring at me lustfully, before he shook his head. He unhooked my bra, pulled it off, and then ripped my thong off like he always does. He placed soft kisses all over my body, stopping at my nipples to suck on them, and then kissing down my stomach to my dripping wet honey pot. Phoenix started to eat my pussy so good that I had no choice but to turn my legs into some ear muffs for him. The faster he flicked his tongue on my clit, the faster my body shook, and I knew that I was getting ready to lose it.

"Phoeeniixxxx, daddy! Ohhh my Godddd!" I squealed as I came in his mouth.

When he got up, my whole body went limp from that orgasm that he brought my body to. He got undressed, and his dick was oozing with pre-cum. Before he could straddle me, I got off the bed and got on my knees. I took his dick in both of my hands, and started sucking it the best that I could. He reached down and took my neck in his hand. You know how you hold an apple? That's how he was gripping my neck. Gently, he started to fuck my face. He truly knew how to take control. After he instructed me to tighten my jaws up, he went up on his tiptoes and started moaning.

"Fuck, lil' woman! You're so beautiful. You'll be even more beautiful with my cum dripping off your face. Can daddy nut on your pretty little face?"

Whew! I ain't never had cum in my mouth, let alone my face, but sucking his thick dick turned me on, so I would have agreed to anything.

He removed his hand from my neck and gripped a handful of my hair, yanking my head back.

"Open your mouth, baby," he whispered.

I followed his instructions, and he sprayed a little of his nut into my mouth, and then turned my head from side to side, shooting the rest of it on my face. He closed his eyes and shook his head.

"Girl, you got me all fucked up in the head," he said. "I don't like this shit, for real."

He went and got me a towel to clean my face off. He pulled me up on my feet and laid me on the bed. Without warning, he entered me, and I gasped as he filled me up with his manhood. I closed my eyes as I let Phoenix take my body to ecstasy while Keith Sweat and Kut Klose's voices filled the room.

"Look at me, Kam, damn it!" he ordered. "You been giving this pussy away, huh?"

I shook my head, and he hooked my legs in his arms and started giving me long and very deep strokes, making my eyes roll in the back of my damn head.

"Damn right! Who this pussy belongs to? Let me mothafuckin' know! I can't hear you, Kambridge!"

"Phhoeenixx Bailey! My pussy belongs to Phoenix Baileyyy!" I screamed out.

"Shit! That's what I like to hear! Tell the world, baby!"

The harder he hit the bottom of my pussy, the deeper I dug my nails in his chest and back. He moaned while I was digging my nails in his skin, and he threw his head back like he enjoyed the pain. His strokes slowed down when Jesse's Powell song "You" came on. Our eyes were dead locked on each other like if we blinked we would miss something.

"Kambridge, I love you, mama," he whispered.

"I love you, too, Phoenix Bailey," I whispered back to him.

"Can I give you a shorty? I want a family with you. Can I cum in you?"

"Ain't you been cumming in me?"

"Yeah, but that's beside the point, and don't fuck the mood up. Answer me. Can I give you my shorty?"

I gripped his face with both of my hands, and replied, "Yes, daddy! I want your baby."

Five minutes later, both of us came so hard that we were stuck in place momentarily. After we gained feelings in our lower half, we got up and showered together. I was putting my clothes back on so I could go home because it was getting close to my curfew.

"Kam, can you stay with me tonight?" he asked.

"You know I can't stay. My dad would kill me," I replied.

I hadn't stayed over here before. Every time I would fall asleep, I would set an alarm for thirty minutes before my curfew, so I could get home.

"Mane, if your dad put his hands on you again, I will rock his ass. I mean that shit. I'm your man, I will protect you. Please stay with me. I'm begging you," he said with his hands clasped together.

His begging face was too cute not to say no. I got undressed and climbed in the bed with him. I got excited at the thought of sleeping on his chest all night instead of just a couple of hours. I would just have to deal with my dad tomorrow.

Malice

Waking up with Kam's naked body on my naked body had to be one of the best feelings in the world. Last night, we talked, fucked, and repeated that sequence a couple of times before we eventually drifted off to sleep. I slept in the bed with Cat plenty of times, but it had never been this intimate. She slept on one side, and I slept on the other side. I looked down at Kam, and it was as if she is holding on to me as if I was going to leave her in the middle of the night or something.

Prying Kam's arms away from around me was kind of hard, but the minute I did, she turned over. I slowly slid out of the bed and covered her back up. I went to the bathroom to relieve my bladder, and rolled up a blunt. I walked on the roof so I could smoke. This shit was stressing me out bad because I wanted to be Kam's man, but I knew that I truly couldn't give her all of me right now.

The two weeks I wasn't talking to her, I wasn't fucking with her mama, if that's what you were thinking. I blocked her ass, but she kept texting me and calling me from phone apps, trying to meet up with me. She told me that she wouldn't tell Kam, and that shit bothered me to my soul. She knew that I was fucking her daughter, but she still tried to get on this dick. That shit was over with. These last two weeks had been crazy as shit without her, but I needed a moment to step back and think. At first, I thought that she was going to tell Kam, so that was my initial reason for leaving her alone, but when her mom kept calling my phone, I knew that she had never told her.

"You just couldn't stay away, huh?" my brother asked me as he stepped out puffing on his own blunt.

"I tried, but two weeks was long enough. She was invading my mind so bad, bro. Her mom keep calling me from phone apps trying to get me to come fuck her. This woman talking about she will pay me double to get my dick. I mean, I know the shit worth it, but what type of mama is she? First, she is cheating on her husband, but now she's trying to continue to fuck me, knowing that I'm beating her daughter's walls down," I said.

"Bro, you gotta tell lil' mama. It's going to hurt, and she may even stop fucking with you, but I'm telling you, it's going to hurt much less coming from you. You already saying Cat on some real fatal attraction type shit. Honestly, leave all that shit alone and just gon' head and work with me. Don't look at me like that. Just take over for Kade until you get your shop up and running after he quits," he spoke.

"What you mean after he quits?" I asked.

"That mane ain't gon' work with me after shit hit the fan with lil' mama in there," he said, rubbing his hand down his curly fro.

He took a few more puffs on his blunt, put it out, and walked back in the house. I took a few more puffs on mine, and then followed him in the house. I peeked my head in the room, and my lil' woman was still laying in the bed. She was holding on to that pillow for dear life. I walked in the kitchen to start cooking her breakfast. I pulled out the breakfast food and spread it out on the counter. Mayhem was sitting at the table, looking at me crazy.

"What, nigga?" I asked.

"Love make you do crazy shit, and I don't want no parts of that type of shit," he said, shaking his head. "Your ass ain't never cooked no damn breakfast. Now you in here about to burn our house down for shorty."

"Whatever, nigga."

"Nah, don't whatever me, but I'm sure after all that fucking y'all did last night, she need to refuel. '*Phoenix Bailey, it's yourrsss,*'" he mocked Kam.

"Damn, you used to leave early and come in late. Now you here every time she's here. You got something you need to tell me? You getting off on me fucking my girl or something, ol' weird ass nigga?"

"Hell naw! She be so loud, the whole damn neighborhood can hear her, what you mean? She spent the whole night, nigga, and I came in early."

I laughed at his dumb ass and started cooking for my woman. I pulled my ringing phone out my pocket, and answered it without looking at it.

"Malice," I answered.

"Is my daughter with you? Her father is looking for her, and I just need to know if she is over there?" Tracey whispered into the phone, and I could tell that she was in the bathroom or somewhere.

I looked at the number, and it was from one of those phone app numbers that I was going to block when I hung up the phone. I'm sure

I had about fifteen blocked numbers that Tracey had been calling me from.

"You don't give a damn where she's at. You just ain't expect me to pick up. Stop calling me, for real."

"I'm serious. Is she with you? Her dad is fussing. That's why I'm whispering into the phone. We been calling her, and she ain't picking up."

"Look, I ain't crazy. Right now, it's 7:52 in the morning, and you leave for work at 8:15. You check on Kam at 8:00 in the morning before you leave for work, and her dad don't check on her at all. Don't fucking play with me."

I wasn't paying attention to what she was saying while I walked to my room and looked at Kam's phone. She has no missed calls, and I placed a kiss on her sleeping forehead before I left out the room.

"I just looked at Kam's phone, and there are no missed calls from y'all. Don't call me again," I snapped and hung up the phone.

I blocked the number so she wouldn't be able to call me again. Before I could even set my phone down again, there was a message.

847-679-0989: I'll pay you two thousand dollars just to let me suck your dick, please. My husband is just... please, Malice. You know Kambridge is not making you come out the seat like I do!!!!!!! PLEASE! Just one last time.

How the fuck did she make a new phone number that fast? I shook my head before I deleted the message and put my phone back in my pocket. Tracey could suck a meannn dick, but my lil' woman was learning, so I wasn't even mad. I was just glad that I could be able to teach her.

I had just finished cooking breakfast, when she appeared in the doorway with my t- shirt on that swallowed her little body.

"Good morning, Phoenix, and you must be Mayhem. I'm sorry that we have never met before," Kam said, walking towards him with her small hand held out. He stood, shook her hand, and then sat back down. "I've heard so much about you, Mr. Mayhem," she said, and sat down at the table across from him.

"What you heard about my brother?" I asked curiously.

"Um, Shelly talks about how fine he is, and she didn't lie. You guys look identical to each other," Kam laughed.

Me and him looked at each as we always do when we get that statement. We didn't think we looked alike.

"Oh, lil' white shorty. She too young for me. I'm thirty years old, and even if I was slightly interested in her, she is doing too much to get my attention. Fucking my niggas ain't gon' get my attention," Mayhem said to Kam.

She shrugged off what he was saying, and then she turned back to me and smiled.

"You cooked all this for me? I am so grateful because I sure am hungry, but I have to eat and run. I have an order to go mail off, and then I have a full schedule this morning. I was only going to close my store for half a day. Then I have to get a change of clothes from my house, and⬚"

"Kam, slow down," I said because she was getting ready to run her brain ragged trying to remember everything that she had to do this morning. "Can I come with you? My next class don't start until two weeks from now."

"It's a bunch of girl stuff. You wouldn't⊠"

"Kam, I want to come," I said.

She laughed and then looked at Mayhem. "You see how niggas are. Now this time next year, he'll be shooing me away to go do girl shit by myself. Niggas will do any and everything to get you, but won't do any and everything to keep you. Ain't that a shame, Mayhem?"

"Fuck it then," I said, slamming her plate down in front of her. "I ain't gotta go."

"Oh shut up. You can come. Just don't say I didn't warn you, and we are going in the same car so you won't leave me."

I smirked at her before I fixed my plate to join her at the table. I could barely eat because I was watching her lips wrap around the fork. Kam is so beautiful, and I hope that she knew that. Her body was so soft, and everything with her felt right.

"You're so creepy, Phoenix," she whispered, breaking my trance. "Eat your food before it gets cold. I'm going to go take a shower and raid your closet. I have to go to my car first though."

She got up, washed her plate, and walked out the kitchen. I heard her go outside and come back in.

"Boy, you got it bad for that girl. You should have seen the way you were staring at her. You were getting lost in her. It was like she was stealing your soul right out of your eyeballs. She was taking your breath away, and she wasn't even looking at you," Mayhem said.

"I like looking at her," I replied.

"Malice, you need to be careful, honestly. You're falling hard and too fast in my opinion. This is the first relationship you have had outside of your… you know, and I don't want you to be blinded and you end up getting hurt or something like that," he said.

I continued to listen to my brother talk about Kam's and my relationship, or whatever we got going on, but it was going in one ear and out the other. I'd end up hurting her before she hurts me.

∞

"Kam, what's a deal breaker for you?" I asked as we headed to her store.

I looked at her, and she was looking good as fuck. She had on one of my t-shirts that was too small for me, and a pair of open-toe heels that she had in the trunk of her car. She had put two braids in the front of her hair, and had gelled the rest of it up into a big poof on top of her head. Her makeup was flawless. I told her she didn't have to wear it, but you know how she is.

"What does that mean?" she asked. "Like, what I will and won't put up with in a relationship?"

I nodded my head.

"I definitely won't put up with cheating and disrespect. Disrespect as in talking to me how you wouldn't talk to your mom, or whoever you respect. You talk to me respectful, and I'll return it. Don't cheat on me, because I won't cheat on you. That's just simple. Please break up with me if you want to cheat. I wish men all over the world could understand that."

"Women cheat too," I said, thinking about all the married women I have fucked.

"That's true too, but that ain't what we are talking about. We are talking about men."

"Yeah, yeah, yeah, you want the heat off y'all cheating ass women."

"How did we even get on that to begin with? You were asking me about my deal breakers. We will get to yours in a minute, but I think that's it though. Don't cheat and don't disrespect. I will probably get some more as the relationship grows, but for right now, that's all I got. Now, what are yours?"

"Honestly, I think that's all I got as well. I ain't never been in a solid relationship to know what my deal breakers are. Don't cheat on me, and treat me the same way I treat you."

We pulled up to her store, and I got out to get the boxes from the back so we could go to the post office. I put the boxes in the back seat of the car, and got back in the driver's seat. I drove off and headed toward the nearest post office.

"You know, I don't mean to be in your business, but why haven't you been in any type of relationship? You are damn near thirty. I expected you to be in at least two or three serious relationships by now."

"Um, good question. I don't know. I guess I can say that I really ain't just ran into anybody that's worth getting to know past a good fuck and goodbye. Then you got girls who try to get with you because of who you are. Then you got girls who try to get with you because you got money. I can usually spot those types of women from a mile away," I said as I pulled up to the post office.

"How you know I'm not one of those women?" she asked and got out the car to get the boxes out the back seat.

As she switched her hips into the post office, I pondered on that question she asked me. She runs her own store, which means that she has her own money, and she clearly didn't know who I was when I first walked in her store. Plus, I was only getting to know her because of my dad, but now, I liked her. I loved her, even. She was different. Her conversation was different. That's how I knew she was not one of those women.

When she got back in the car, she pressed the next location into the GPS, and it was right around the corner. She turned the music up and started bobbing her head to The Deele's "Two Occasions." I turned the music down, and she looked at me crazy.

"You have good taste in music. Where did that come from and you are only twenty-two years old?"

"Well, my dad's records. I don't know if you remember seeing the record player in the corner of my basement, but I play my dad's records on it. Also, I practice playing my violin to the songs, so that's pretty much all I listen to. Kalena puts me on to the new school music."

We rode for ten minutes before we pulled into Wax Labs. We got out the car, walked inside the building, and she wrote her name down on the piece of paper. She took a seat next to me and started reading the magazine.

"Kammmmy, girll! I was getting ready to call you," a short black girl said from the door. "You can come on back," she said.

"Malice, you coming back with me?"

I shrugged and got up to follow her. The minute she walked in the room, Kambridge started getting undressed. I leaned against the wall.

"Aye, don't she supposed to leave while you get undressed or something?" I asked Kam.

"Aysha has been seeing my body since I was eighteen, so we are good," Kam replied. "Oh, Aysha, that's⊠"

"Malice Bailey. Everyone knows who he is. What are you doing with him, is the question, girl? Spill the fucking piping hot tea," Aysha cut off the introduction.

Aysha poured powder on Kam's pussy, and then spread wax on it. Kam didn't even flinch when she snatched the wax off, but I did. That shit looked painful.

"Well, girl, Malice and I are friends. Really good friends," she smirked.

"Biiitttchhhh, this nigga took your V card. Damn! Girl, how was it?"

"Girl, it was everything I imagined it would be, and now I can't get enough of him."

"Okay, ladies, can you stop talking about me like I'm not standing right here?" I interrupted their girl talk, and they both looked at me with an attitude. I held my hands up in surrender mode.

"Girl, since he got an attitude, you can text me and catch me up. Let me catch you up with me. These messy ass bitches here damn near about to make me quit my job. I swear if I had somewhere else to go, I would be out of here."

"Well, you will have somewhere else to go soon. If you can just hang on for about six months to a year, Rich Cutz will be opening, and it will have all types of people in there. It's kind of like a hood beauty bar or something like that. You can get your hair cut, slayed, manicures, pedicures, Brazilians, facials, and everything else that us women need," Kambridge said.

"Where that's going to be at, and why I have to wait so long?"

"Well, because Malice hasn't opened it yet, but I promise you when he does, you are going to be the first person I call. But his shop is going to be popping, so you'll have to bring a couple more people with you."

Aysha and Kam continued to have girl talk while she got her legs and underarms waxed, and all I could think about was the fact that my baby girl was doing more recruiting than I had done. I hadn't talked to anyone yet, because I was just trying to get my building first. After that, I was going to start hiring people. When Kam was done, we left right out the store.

"Kam, you didn't pay," I said to her.

"I know. It automatically comes out of my bank account once every six weeks. Now we about to go up the street to the nail salon."

"Okay, cool."

"Alright, Malice, the jig is up. What is wrong with you? I know something is wrong with you. You are living good, your money is right, your sex is amazing, and no woman has tried to beat me up yet. You seem too good to be true," Kam said, looking at me while waiting for an answer, but I didn't have one.

"Nothing is wrong with me, Kam. I promise. This is me. I'm not faking or fronting. This is me," I assured her.

"Uh-huh. Let me find out," she laughed.

We pulled up to the nail salon and got out. The moment we stepped in, the women started looking at me with lust in their eyes. Even a couple of my clients were in here. They were married, so I wasn't worried about them saying anything. It was like the whole shop got quiet when we walked in, like they were talking about black people or something. Kam urged me to get a pedicure with her, and like the sap nigga I had become because of her, I did. No sooner than the pedicurist turned the water on, Cat walked her ass in there. She got in the chair right next to me, and I wished that I could disappear.

I kept my head down, looking at the blue water as it covered my feet. I grabbed Kam's hand and kissed it. She looked at me and smiled, and then frowned when she looked past me and saw Cat.

"Small world, huh, Lam?" she said to Kam, being funny.

"It's Kam, actually, and it's Kambridge to you because I don't know you, and yes, it is! I didn't know that you come here. I'm a regular here every week, and I haven't seen you before. I'm sorry, I don't remember your name," Kam smirked.

"Cat. Catherine Jenson."

Kam gave the fakest grin ever and leaned back against the chair. I couldn't even enjoy the pedicure, because Cat being next to me had me heated. I cut my eyes at Kam, and she was laid back, enjoying the massage chair with her eyes closed. My phone vibrated in my pocket, and I already knew who it was.

Cat: What would you do if I told your little girlfriend about us, and about two more women in here?

Me: My other clients will deny it, and I will never fuck with you again.

Cat: You haven't had sex with me since I guess you been having sex with her. So, I don't even care anymore.

I shook my head and put my phone back in my pocket. Cat kept trying to make small talk with me, but I kept ignoring her. I prayed that the pedicure didn't last long, because the longer I sat here, the longer I wanted to crack this bitch upside her head.

Thirty minutes later, we were done, and Kam was done with her girly things for the day. I enjoyed spending time with her, but this would be something that I barely did with her. After driving to the other side of town, I pulled up in front of one of the buildings that I had been looking at. Kam immediately started in on the questions; I knew that she would have reservations about the building's location.

"This is the building you want for your shop? Why you want it over here, and why is this for sale sign still here?" she asked with one of her eyebrows raised.

"Well, yes, this is the building that I want. I want this building because I want it to be in this part of town because I want *my* people to really have somewhere nice to get their beauty shit done, where them pussy ass pigs won't fuck with us. Even though it's in this part of town, the owner trying to sell this building for two hundred racks. Two hundred. He only doing that because I ain't trying to rent shit. I could have easily bought this building for seventy-five racks."

"Well, how much you got now? Can we go inside?"

"Nah, but I have a video of the inside of the building. I have about two hundred saved up, but if I spend it all on the building, then I won't have enough to fix it up all at one time, and buy all the equipment."

"Well, I can have the person who did my store come and look to see what can be done. He will give you a discount because he fucks with my dad, and I have a pretty penny saved up, and I can let you borrow the money. Also, you can find different websites that offer discounts on different types of seats and stuff. I'm so excited to get this place up and running, Phoenix. It's going to be amazing."

"Nah, Kam. I can't take thousands of dollars from you like that. I swear that it won't even feel right. It makes me so happy that you are excited. You make me ready to open this bitch tomorrow. Everybody was already fucking with the jerseys and shit, so I know I'll have a lot of business."

"We'll be business partners. Consider it our first partner deal," she said and shot me a smile. "Also, you can have a barbeque, or whatever you guys eat over here, and pass out fliers once it gets close to opening night just..."

"Wait, what you mean, '*or whatever you guys eat over here.*' You are acting like you don't eat BBQ," I cut her off, looking at her crazy.

Her eyes darting from side to side and her shrugging, let me know the obvious. This girl really needed to experience this side of Chicago. We might have to stay with one of the homeboys in the projects one night. She needed to hear some gunshots.

"I'm sorry. I have never had it before. Maybe you can barbeque for me while we go over this business plan," she offered.

I pulled her into a huge embrace, and then placed sweet kisses on her lips. I couldn't believe that this girl was doing this for me. There was really no way that I could repay her for this. Every time she did something nice for me, my heart swelled and then instantly deflated because I knew that one day I was going to hurt her so bad, and I didn't want to.

Cat

*M*alice had life completely twisted up if he thought that he was just going to get over on me and ride off into the sunset with that young ass bitch. Last night, I was parked down the road from Malice's house, and her car was in his yard. It was there all night. I fell asleep in my car, waiting for that bitch to leave his house, but she didn't. When I woke up, her car was still there, and I could feel my body getting hot all over. She came out the house, and I could see her glowing from where I was parked.

Yeah, that's what Malice's dick do to you, make you glow, whore, I thought to myself.

I can't believe that I had been sitting here for hours before they came out the house, hand-in-hand to her car. I followed they asses all over the city, stopping at every place they went, and then into the nail salon. I couldn't help myself, because I had to let Malice know that this was a very dangerous game that he was playing. The look on his face was priceless when he saw me.

As soon as they were done and out the door, I jumped out the water, feet undone, and threw the lady the cash. I rushed out to the car and sped off behind them. They stopped in front of a building and got out. I watched them. I studied them. They had to be talking about something important because Malice always stroked his beard when he was thinking. The way he was with her was different. He was kissing all over her and carrying on like they were two horny teenagers, and I got sick to my stomach. After they drove off, I pulled up to the building and saw the building was for sale, and that the realtor's name was Bernie Green. I pulled my phone out and took a picture of the sign.

"I got something for Malice if he thinks that he is going to fuck with me." I laughed to myself.

I sped home, pulled out my account books, and called Mr. Bernie Green. He picked up on the first ring.

"Bernie Green Realty," he spoke into the phone.

"My name is Catherine Jenson, and I would like to purchase the building that you have on Second Street. How much is it? I am ready to purchase today," I said while flipping through my account books.

"I'm actually saving that building for a client. I'm sorry," he said.

"How much is that person paying?" I asked.

"The building is costing two hundred thousand dol⊠"

"I'll give you three hundred right now…today," I offered.

"You have to come into my office so we can⊠"

"DONE!" I said and hung up the phone.

I got up to take a much-needed shower before I went to sign on the dotted line, to dismantle Malice's little plan. The whole time I was in the shower, I was thinking about how I was going to have Malice in the palm of my hand again. I knew how bad he wanted that building because he used to talk about it every day. He told me that he was looking at a couple more, but that is the one that he really wanted.

After I got out the shower, I put on my clothes and headed to Mr. Green's business. On the way there, I hoped and prayed that this worked because if it didn't, then I was going to have to go to extreme measures which wouldn't be limited to telling his little girlfriend about his real job, or unscrewing the lug nuts on a tire. I still had the photos of Malice and his clients coming out of hotels, and I even spiced it up and added our videos to the collection. Well, he didn't know that I recorded us, but I did. I loved to watch him sliding in and out of me, and the way his face twisted up when he's getting ready to cum. There were times when Malice fucked me silly, and there were times when Malice made love to me, or at least I thought it was making love.

When I pulled up to Bernie Green's Realty, I got out my car, smoothed my skirt down, and walked in the building with my head held high. There were three men in the waiting area, and I already knew which one was Bernie. All the Bernies I knew were shaped like a little stump with a bad toupee, and the guy that was approaching me was shaped just like that.

"Hey, I'm Bernie, you must be Catherine?" he asked with his sweaty looking hand held out.

I nodded my head, and he instructed me to follow him into his office. We sat at the round table, which was full of paperwork. For the next two hours, we signed paperwork, called the bank, verified who I was, and everything else he needed so I could get the keys to the building. After everything was done, I made him a high ass commission, and I held the key to all of Malice's hopes and dreams.

Kam

$\mathcal{S}$itting next to a nervous Phoenix, who has never flown before, was driving me insane with the 'what-ifs.' I'm sure I would lose my mind if I heard him start another sentence with 'what-if.' Since his last class before he got his Bachelor's started in a couple of weeks, we decided to take our trip to St. Maarten. After they called the priority fliers, we scanned our tickets and took our seats in the first-class section. I had never seen Phoenix sweat as much as he was sweating right now. His brand new white t-shirt was soaking wet.

"Phoenix Bailey, if you don't get your damn act together, they are going to kick you off the flight. You will be okay," I assured him.

"That's easy for you to say, Kambridge Lewis. You have been on a hundred flights," he hissed while wiping the sweat off his top lip.

The flight attendant approached us to get our drink order. I ordered Phoenix a glass of Patrón and ordered myself some water. When you rode in first class, you could get a drink before everyone even got in their seats.

"Ooowwweee Lord, help me. They serve alcohol on this bitch! We finna die. What if☒"

I placed my hand over his mouth before he finished his statement because I was 'what if'd' out.

"Phoenix, put your seat belt on and sit back. You are embarrassing me. We are going to be okay. Trust me." I took his sweaty hands in mine and kissed them. "I promise you."

The flight attendant brought us our drinks, and he damn near snatched the drink out of her hand to gulp the drink down. He asked for another one, but I shook my head to the flight attendant. Phoenix's ass didn't drink like that, and his ass would end up drunk if he had another glass. The flight attendant started going over the instructions for the exit door, seat belt, and oxygen mask. I kept looking at Phoenix out the corner of my eye, and I could tell that he was getting anxious because he was grabbing the armrests tightly. I couldn't think of anything to calm him down, so I pulled the blanket over us and started massaging his dick through his sweats. Thank God it was a late flight, so the plane was slightly dark and you had to be staring real hard to see what I was doing. We were sitting on the runway, getting ready to take off, and I didn't need Phoenix to act a fool.

"So, you want to die playing with the dick, huh?" he whispered.

"If I die next to you, that would be just fine with me," I whispered back.

He held his head down and watched me massage his now hard dick. I swear this nigga was so sexual, if that's the right word to use, because if I just touched this nigga, his dick would stand up. I could see him pull his big ass bottom lip in his mouth. The plane was ripping down the runway, getting ready to lift into the air, so I started going faster. I could tell that he was close to cumming because he started moving his hips as best he could.

"You about to cum for mama, ain't you?" I whispered in his ear.

I reached into his pants, not missing a beat with jacking off his dick.

He nodded his head up, and down real fast.

"Make this dick cum for me then! This my dick, ain't it?" I whispered, and then bit his earlobe.

As his dick started pulsating, his breath quickened, and he released all over his thigh. I pulled my hand out of his pants just as the flight attendant came to give me more water. I asked her for napkins so he could reach in his pants and clean himself up.

"Thank you, I needed that," he said to me. "It's not so bad up here." He slid the window cover up to look out the window.

"I told you. Now, are you a ready for a twelve-hour flight to China?" I joked.

"Hell nah. Let me get past these four hours first, and then we might can talk. I mean well, if I can get that 'take-off' treatment again, then I'll be ready for any flight," he laughed.

Between that drink and that hand job, Phoenix was knocked out not even an hour into the flight. Since I wasn't sleepy, I used that time to look up all the different types of chairs that we were going to need for Rich Cutz. I was so excited to be taking this venture alongside him. When he talked about Rich Cutz, his face lit up, and I could tell that he really was going to be a great business owner. I knew the average person would say that it was too early to be making such a huge and dangerous jump, but Phoenix was so determined, and I felt in my heart that this was going to work. I was a little upset that the building was as expensive as it was, because nothing in that area looked like it cost that much; no offense, though. I wished that I could get my dad to talk to the owner of the building so he could take the price down because the building was not even worth two hundred dollars. It's going to be once Phoenix and I were done with the building. One question that kept bothering me was how he managed to save up two hundred thousand dollars if he didn't sell drugs or none of that. I knew he ain't saved up that type of money cutting hair. I was kind of afraid to even know the answer.

I glanced over at Phoenix, and he looked so peaceful when he slept. I liked that when I slept on his chest that our heartbeats were identical to one another. We hadn't put a title yet on what we have; it's not a relationship, but it's more than friends. One might think that we are moving too fast, but I think we are moving at the right pace. The main person who thought we were moving too fast was my mom. I already knew my dad's opinion. I told my mom, Kade, and Kalena that I was going on vacation with Phoenix, and she lost it. She was telling me that he was going to hurt me, and he wasn't good enough for me, and how I needed to get back with Connor. When she told me that, I almost had a low-grade heart attack. I knew my mom and dad didn't like Connor, because he was white, but they didn't voice it as much, and they didn't treat him any differently. So why she told me that she would prefer me to be with Connor, I would never know, and I wasn't going to ask. I didn't tell my dad that I was going on vacation with Phoenix, but he knew I was going.

My dad's and my relationship has been … different. I think that's the only way that I could explain it right now. He hadn't hit me in a while, and it was almost weird. I was so prepared to get my ass stomped out when I finally made it home from spending the night with Phoenix, and surprisingly, he even brought me lunch. Well, it was breakfast that my mom made for me, but I wasn't there. Her ass hadn't even cooked breakfast in a long time, so that was weird too. He had snuck in my room, while I was napping, and put it on my nightstand along with a note telling me that he was sorry. What the fuck was going on with my family? I don't know, but if no one was getting abused and my dad was not asking me about Malice's family, I wouldn't question it anymore. I have to be tired to go to sleep on an airplane, so I stayed up to get my email blasts ready for the upcoming sale that I was getting ready to have.

∞

Waiting at baggage claim, I could tell that Phoenix wasn't as nervous as I thought he would be. When the plane was landing, I woke him up, and he didn't even overact like he did when he first got on the plane. Once we got out our luggage, we headed toward the exit of the airport. We approached our driver that was holding our name card.

"Mr. and Mrs. Phoenix Bailey, huh?" he asked. "Speak that shit into existence then, mama!" he said.

When he looked down at me, he winked, and I swear if I was white, I would have turned pink. This man was truly doing something to me. He was so smart, loved me for me, and was sexy as fuck. I couldn't even talk about that good dick. The man be fucking me like he came on this earth knowing how to fuck, and it was only getting better. This man could teach a class on fucking and charge a pretty penny. As much I loved anal sex, he hadn't even tried to put his dick in there. He told me that I wouldn't be able to handle it.

We introduced ourselves to the driver, and he said that he would be our driver for the entire duration of our trip. We walked outside to a beautiful black Maybach. He put our luggage in the trunk while we slid in the back seat. The driver got in and headed towards our house for the week. I was taking in the night view of St. Maarten, and it was nice as fuck. Malice's hand creeping up my leg made me look at him. His hand ended up around my neck, and he squeezed, … tight, taking the air right out of my body before he leaned into me.

"For the duration of this trip, … you will be my bitch!" he growled into my ear. "Do you understand me?"

I nodded my head as best as I could. I was so fucking turned on it was crazy. He loosened the grip on my neck, but kept his lips right by my ear.

"You want to be my wife, so I'm going to treat you how I would treat my wife. This week, you will be my sex slave. Whatever I want you to do, you will do, or I will punish you for it. I'm going to fuck you in every room of the house, the patio, the kitchen table, on the stairs; any time my dick gets hard, it's going into a hole on your body… any hole," he said, and then bit my earlobe. "My name is now daddy! Do you understand me?"

"Yes," I managed to whisper.

I could feel my pussy gushing from the way Phoenix was talking to me. He let me go and then placed a sloppy kiss on my lips. I mean sloppy too. He had never kissed me this way. If he would only kiss his wife this way, then I needed to pretend to be his wife more often.

"Mr. and Mrs. Bailey, we are here. There are food places right around the corner if you would like for me to take you around the corner," the driver spoke as we pulled up.

"No, Mr. Parker. We are fine. We will call you if we need you. It seems like there is a lot of shit in this area, so we may not need you as much," Phoenix said to him.

He opened the door for us and got our luggage out the trunk. We tipped him, and Phoenix led the way into our house. The place was amazing. It was three bedrooms and two bathrooms. There was a game room, a small theater, and a small pool out back. The house was perfect for a family of four or five. I fell in love instantly.

"This house is perfect!" I said as I fell onto the king-sized bed in the master bedroom.

"Hell yeah, this shit is dope as fuck. I'm getting something like this for my family one day," he said as he slid our luggage into the closet.

"How big of a family do you want to have?" I asked, while staring at the pretty chandelier.

"Well, I always wanted a family, I knew that. I even knew that I wanted to get married, but I ain't know if I wanted to have kids or not, until I met you. I want to see you pregnant." He walked over to me and started rubbing on my stomach. "I want to see you dragging my little shorty around in your belly while cursing me out for getting you pregnant, and telling me that I ain't never getting you pregnant again. After we have our first one, we will go from there."

"What kind of father would you be?"

"Um, I'm going to be the man that my father should have been, not trying to force my kid to do anything that he doesn't want to do.

I'm going to support my kid in anything that they want to do, whether it's dancing, playing basketball, or being a fucking yoga instructor. I'm going to be behind them one hundred per-fucking-cent," he snapped.

I could tell that while he was talking to me, his mind went somewhere else. His jaw muscles were clenching, and he started clenching his hands tightly into fists. I slightly covered his hands on his clenched fists.

"Baby, talk to me," I whispered. "What's going on?"

He laid next to me, with his hands clasped together behind his head, looking at the ceiling.

"Your dad hates you, but my dad hates me too. Not as much as your dad hates you. He's never abused me or any of that, but he did treat me differently. See, Kambridge … can you promise me something?" he asked.

"Yeah, anything."

"Look me in my eyes, and promise me that you won't tell anyone about this conversation I'm about to have with you."

I looked at him, and promised him that the conversation wouldn't go any further than this bedroom.

"My dad is a drug dealer. My brother is a drug dealer, and I tried that shit only for a little while and realized that it wasn't for me. My dad has been pressuring me to get in the game since I was a teenager. That's why our names are Mayhem and Malice. We were supposed to be the Bailey brothers who ran the whole city, but after being in the streets for a little while, I knew that it was not for me. My dad only did the bare minimum for me. Only giving me things that I needed. If it wasn't for my uncle Trent, I wouldn't have had half of the shit that I had. I'm going to take you to meet him. He's in jail. He was arrested when I was seven years old. He's been in there for twenty-two years. We still talk like he's on the outside though."

Oh, so that's how he has been able to save up that two hundred thousand dollars, I thought to myself.

"See, your mom is much like mom. Let my dad get away with the shit. She wasn't going nowhere. At least your mom could have got you away from that shit. A part of me thinks that's why I got so attached to you so fast. You give me what I've been missing my whole entire life. Real love. Attention. Help. I truly feel like you are my other half. I find myself praying for you, Kambridge. I haven't prayed in a long time. I just pray that you keep that beautiful smile on your face. I pray that your heart continues to get bigger. I even pray that I get my shit together enough to be able to call myself your boyfriend one day. You deserve better than the Malice I am today. I'm going to work my ass off to give you everything you deserve, and more. You're perfect, Kambridge Lewis, and I swear to God, you are going to be Mrs. Phoenix Allen Bailey."

"Your middle name is Allen?" I snickered.

"Whatever. Enough of this mushy shit. Let's go get something to eat," he said.

I couldn't front and say that my heart was not full after Phoenix's speech, because it was beating so hard that it damn near jumped out of my chest. Phoenix was always expressing himself, but I never expected him to say what he said a few moments ago. I didn't even expect him to tell me about his dad being a drug dealer. Even though I knew because of what my dad said to me, I was still shocked to hear it come out of his mouth. I wasn't going to open my mouth about any of it. Phoenix needed to know that someone was in his corner, and that person was me. I wasn't going to break our promise. My dad was just going to have to beat me every day, and for Phoenix, I would gladly take it.

Malice

$\mathcal{R}$egardless of what Mayhem said about not letting Kam into my family business, I felt comfortable opening up to my woman about my family and the way they felt about me. I felt like by the end of this trip, I would tell her that I was a male escort and just the let the chips fall where they may.

After we changed our travel clothes, we headed out to find the nearest open place to eat. My stomach was damn near touching my back. Kam had put on a maxi dress with some sandals, and I was throwing on some shorts and a white tee. While I was changing, I could see Kam in my peripheral, staring me down. She ain't know I was low-key watching her as well. The way she was looking at me now let me know that she wanted some dick. When she was biting that big ass bottom lip, she wanted this monster, but when she just randomly looked at me, she was just admiring me.

"You ready?" I asked her.

"Yes, sir, I am. I been waiting on you. I swear it take you as long as me to get ready sometimes."

"Whatever." I waved her off.

When we walked out our front door, we had a good view of the beach. The night air in St. Maarten felt good as hell, even with us being two steps from the beach. It seemed like the moon was hovering low on the beach, lighting the beach up. I couldn't wait to see it in the daytime. While I was admiring the beach, I looked up and Kam had her arm out, leaning against the sign. I could see her legs buckling, and I rushed to catch her before she could fall.

"Kam, what the fuck is wrong with you? Are you okay?" I asked.

"Yeah, I just felt weak for a second," she whispered. "It just came out of nowhere. I need to eat something. I haven't eaten all day because I was trying to prepare for the trip," she said.

"Nah, Kam. I'm going to take you back in the house, and I'm going to go grab us something to eat. You need to lay down before you end up falling or something, and cracking your head wide open," I reasoned.

"I'm fine!" she snapped.

I raised my eyebrow, and I knew that she didn't see it because it was dark, but I wasn't letting her go, and she didn't look like she was fine. Her body was burning up, and the fact that she snapped at me further let me know that something was going on.

"Kam, baby, what's going? You ain't ever talked to me like this before. You sure you straight?"

"You only been knowing me for a few months. You don't know me," she replied to me. "I said, I'm fine. Now leave me the fuck alone about it."

I closed my eyes and counted to ten so I wouldn't go off on her. This was a side of Kam that I had never seen before, and I knew all this shit wasn't coming from no damn hunger, but if she wasn't going to talk about it, then neither was I. When I opened my eyes, she had teetered several steps in front of me. I ain't catch up to her, but I just stayed a few steps behind her in case her ass got dizzy again.

Luckily, the food shops were only a couple of blocks away. We could see the lights from where we were, but this street was a little dark with only a couple of street lights. Kam was walking with not a care in the world, looking down at her phone, and didn't even notice the suspicious man and woman leaning against the wall. I reached to my hip and took my piece off safety. Oh yeah, I didn't travel nowhere without it. Mayhem told me what I needed to do to travel on the plane with it, and I did. I wasn't about to get hit with the okie-doke in another country. You know it's retarded ass niggas everywhere you go.

The woman started walking towards us, and Kam wasn't even looking. Women ain't ever aware of their surroundings. This is how they asses get kidnapped and shit. I knew it was hard, but you had to be looking around always. I was so glad I ain't had no damn sisters. I caught up to her and grabbed her hand. She looked up at me and put her phone away. I nodded towards the woman, and I felt her tense up and hold my hand tightly.

"Both of y'all can take me home for two hundred dollars," the woman said.

"Bitch, get a real job! We are not about to pay you to fuck. We don't get down like that," Kam snapped at the woman, and she backed away.

So much for telling her that I'm a male escort, I thought to myself.

"A simple, 'no, thank you,' would have been cool, Kam. You ain't have to say all that. You are tripping. I need to hurry up and get some food in your system so you can calm down," I said to her.

"Fuck that!" she sniped.

I felt that shit on a personal level because a job is a job, to be honest, whether it's a sex worker or a fucking pediatrician. We all get paid, and that damn ten thousand dollars or so a week ain't hurting my pockets at all, but after I paid for that damn building, my pockets were going to be hurting until I got it up and running.

After we made it to the burger joint, we ordered and sat down to wait on our food. I decided to pick her brain about the lady back there. I had to know how she truly felt about it.

"Kam, why you snap on that woman like that? You don't think that what she does is a job? She gets paid for it." I glared at her. "A job is a paid position of regular employment."

"I mean, why would you want to have sex ... as a job. As much as I love having sex with you, I still wouldn't want to get paid for it. As a woman, how do you tell your daughter that you fuck people for a living? I mean, you have sex with three and four niggas a day. You go home, and that's all you think about. *I had sex with four niggas today, and what...only brought home a thousand dollars.* That's disgusting to me. Plus, what happens when you want to settle down, and you have to tell your husband that you fucked a hundred guys, ... for money. I don't know. That line of work is just disgusting, but I guess somebody gotta do it. Those are the women that be sleeping with women's husbands. Be taking home AIDS to their wives."

Before I could get in a word about the way she felt about it, she continued her tirade. I felt like I shouldn't have asked her because now

I was starting to feel a certain way about her. I didn't know if it was because I was a male escort, or because of the way she talked about them as if they were scum of the earth. It could be both.

"Man, if my husband ever cheated on me with a prostitute, I would divorce him. Out of all the people you work with, you cheated on me with Taymique, the prostitute. You used our hard-earned coins to get your dick wet by a person who gets this done to her at least five times a day."

"Kam, I love you," I said, throwing her off.

She didn't reply, but started looking through her phone, completely ignoring me. Something was wrong. Something was different. I'm not sure what it was, but this Kam was different, and it was going to bother me until I figured out what the problem was. I pulled my phone out and sent a text to my brother.

Me: Mayhem, do me a huge favor, and get back to me ASAP! Get your computer nigga to look up Kam's medical records. I need to figure out if something is wrong with her. Check everything. Don't leave anything out. Break every firewall. I need to know EVERYTHING!

Mayhem: Ain't you been fucking her raw already? Nigga, if she got something, you got it already.

Me: That ain't what I'm looking for. She is being snappy, and this is not her.

Mayhem: Nigga, she a woman. They all are all... nigga don't ever text me using the word snappy, but I'll do that for you. Glad you let a nigga know you landed safely. Thought ISIS had already got you.

Me: Shut up, nigga, that's the only word that I could think of to describe how she was being. Text me the information in the morning. Love ya, family.

Mayhem: *Love you, fam. Peace.*

They had called our name for our food, and I got up to grab it. Kam followed close behind me. We walked back to the house in silence. We didn't even see the man and the woman while we were walking back to the house, which was a good thing. In the house, we ate in silence as well. Well, I ate, and Kam looked like she was picking over her food. I was not used to this Kam. I was used to Kam jumping all over me, and kissing on me. Kam was full of life, conversation, and jokes. She is none of that right now, so I needed to get away from her for a moment.

After I finished eating, I got in the shower. As I was standing under the hot water, I thought about Kam and how much I loved her. Not counting me sleeping with her mother, would she ever accept me for being a male escort? Could she look past that and see me for the person that she fell in love with, or would she hold that over my head? Would she accept me fucking her mother and her during the same time, but not knowing that Tracey was her mother? From everything that she said tonight at the burger joint, she wouldn't forgive me for sleeping with her mother, nor would she forgive me for the way I get money. Fuck!

I scrubbed my body from head to toe, rinsed off, and scrubbed again. I stayed in the shower, I know for close to thirty minutes. I silently prayed that my woman would be in a better mood because I came here to fuck and see the beach, not argue. I pulled my briefs on, and walked back out into the room to see Kam laid back on the bed asleep. She didn't even finish her food. The half-eaten burger was sitting on her chest, and the drink was getting ready to slip out of her hand. I caught the drink just before it was getting ready to hit the carpet. I took the burger off her chest and put it on the nightstand.

Her body looked like it was trembling a little bit, so I pressed my index and middle finger on her neck to check her pulse, and her heart was beating rapidly. I shook her to wake her up. One of her eyes popped open, and then the other one. It was almost as if the light was hurting her eyes. I walked across the room and turned the light off.

"Kam, your heart rate is skyrocketing. Please tell me what's going on," I said to her.

"Right now, I have a headache out of this world," she said, and I started massaging her temples. "They come and go. They started happening right around the time after you left my house. I will have a headache today, be good for a few days, and then have another headache like three days later. I don't think I'm stressed out or nothing. The dizziness came out of nowhere too. Right now, I just want to sleep," she whispered.

"Alright, baby! We need to make you a doctor's appointment. Ain't shit about that normal, a'ight? We can fly back tonight if you want. Why you ain't been said nothing about this to me?"

She shrugged her shoulders and her eyes closed. I undressed her and put her under the cover. I walked to the other side of the bed and got in behind her. I snuggled up behind her and wrapped my arm around her tiny little waist.

"I love you too, Phoenix Allen Bailey." She chuckled lightly, and I pinched her stomach, making her giggle harder.

There was my Kam, I thought to myself before I drifted off to sleep.

∞

When I woke up, I stretched my arm out, and Kam was no longer in bed. I got up and walked into the kitchen. Kam was butt-naked, fixing us breakfast. Her hair was no longer in her large natural curls all over her head, but it was straight down her back. It stopped right in the middle of her back. My dick started swelling in my briefs. Everything about her was so fucking sexy right now. I wanted to skip breakfast and fuck her.

"Good morning, Mrs. Bailey," I announced my presence in the kitchen.

When she turned to look at me, her hair flipped over into her face, and she looked sexy as fuck. Kam's body was a work of art. Her back had scars, but to me it was art, and I loved touching them. She didn't even flinch when I touched her anymore. It was like she welcomed me touching her scars now.

"Good morning, Mr. Bailey. Breakfast is ready. Come have a seat," she said.

"How did you get food, and why didn't you wake me? I could have helped cooked breakfast. You are always on your feet when you work. I wanna take care of you sometimes."

"Baby, I had Mr. Parker go grab us some breakfast foods as soon as the stores opened. If I'm Mrs. Bailey, then I'm going to cook for my husband every other morning, and we can take turns. How about that?" she bargained.

"That will work just fine for me," I said as I took a seat at the table.

Kam set a plate in front of me, and then placed hers on the other side of the table. She went back to the counter to fix us something to drink.

"Girl, what you know about mimosas?" I asked.

"Well, Mr. Parker told me about these drinks, and I told him to pick up the items. I made myself a small glass, and it was good. So, I'm glad that you know about these drinks already," she said as she set our champagne glasses on the table.

She sat down, and we started eating.

"Phoenix, about last night. I don't know what was going on with me. It had to be the headache and the hunger at the same time. I wasn't trying to sound mean regarding the prostitute. I still feel the same way about it, but I know I could have said it in a much nicer way. I could tell that your attitude changed when I was talking mean. That's not me. I'm so sorry," she apologized.

"It's okay, Mrs. Bailey. I know that wasn't you. I know I just need to keep food in your system."

Her huge smile damn near made her eyes close. I guess she loved when I called her that.

"So, when you cook breakfast, am I to look forward to you cooking naked, or even walking around naked?"

"Boy, yes! Well, I'm very comfortable with you, as you can tell, so I will always be naked now. You make me feel so loved, and I'm so grateful for you."

Fuck this! I can't sit across from her any longer because my dick was about to jump out of my damn briefs. I got up from the table and went into the bedroom to get some things from my bag. When I walked back into the kitchen, Kam was just downing the last of her drink, and then finished mine. I smirked because that mimosa was about to have her ass tipsy as fuck. I set the things on the table, and I could see the wheels turning in her head.

I gripped her neck and stood her up.

"Open your mouth," I commanded. "Hold your tongue out as far as it can go."

I opened the spray, and sprayed the back of her throat.

"What was that?" she asked as she popped her lips, trying to see if it had a taste.

"Throat numbing spray. You about to deep throat this dick in a few minutes. Gotta punish you for acting how you was acting last night. I'm about to cum all down your little throat. Get the fuck on your knees."

She followed my instructions and started pulling at the waistband of my briefs. The minute she pulled my briefs down, my damn dick popped up and damn near put her eye out.

"Open your mouth," I ordered. "Stick your tongue out as far as it can go."

I rubbed my dick up and down her tongue, and then pushed my

dick down her throat. Surprisingly, she didn't even gag. She closed her mouth around my dick and started sucking. With the throat numbing spray, she was deep throating my shit with ease. I was turning my little woman into a monster with that throat, and I was falling deeper in love with her looney ass.

"Mrs. Bailey, tighten them jaws up around this dick, and make daddy cum."

She did like I asked her to, and she started getting my dick sloppy wet. Saliva was dripping from her lips, and it was turning me on to the fullest. She gripped my shit with two hands and started doing the two-hand twist, and I went up on my toes because it was feeling so good.

"Fuck, Mrs. Bailey, you about to make me marry the fuck out of you TODAY! Fuckkkk!"

She took one of her hands and started massaging my balls, and that was it. I couldn't take it anymore. I grabbed her hair and started fucking her face, before I came down her throat. I stood her up and started kissing her while backing her up to the counter. I picked her up and placed her on the counter. Luckily, I was tall enough to get on my knees and still be eye length with that pussy. I spread her legs as far as they could go, and her pussy puckered right up for me.

I gave her one long lick up the middle of her slit.

"Keep your eyes on me and your hands on my head, baby. Guide my head wherever you need it to be. A'ight?"

She nodded her head, and I started flicking the tip of my tongue against her clit softly. We kept an intense glare on each other. I pushed two fingers inside of her, and her eyes closed. Pulling my creamy covered fingers out slowly, I placed my fingers in my mouth, and my baby tasted right. My baby was ovulating too, so she was leaving here pregnant.

SMACK!

I smacked her on her ass, and her eyes opened right back up. I put my fingers back inside of her, and tapped on that g-spot, and she creamed my fingers back up again. I raised her off the counter just a little bit, and twirled my tongue around her asshole, and she damn near jumped off the counter. I sat her back down gently.

"A'ight, lil' woman, if you fall and crack your head wide open, I'm not going to have anything to do with that," I chuckled.

Her body was shaking. I walked over to the table, grabbed my other shit, and then walked back over to her. She eyed it and smirked. I stood between her legs, and then hooked them in my arms, and dipped inside of my small piece of heaven. She gasped as I filled her up, and closed her eyes.

"Open your fucking eyes, woman. I want your eyes on me at all times. Don't close them other than to blink, or I'm going to spank you," I ordered.

She wrapped her arms around my neck, and stared at me. It was like we were looking into each other's soul, and my dick was getting even harder.

"Dadddy," she whispered and pulled her big bottom lip into her mouth.

I looked down at my dick going in and out of her, and I had to pull my cream covered dick out of her before I came prematurely. I scooted her down just a little more and placed my dick at the opening of her ass. She gasped when I slid the head of my dick in her. Her cream was all the lubricant I needed as I pushed myself inside of her inch by inch.

"Fuckkkk, Phoenix," she whispered as she struggled to keep her eyes open and on me.

"Who the fuck you call me?" I growled and spanked her cheek hard as I could.

"Dadddy, fuck! I'm sorry! Do that shit again, please!"

I spanked each ass cheek as hard as I could, and her pussy spit out some of the prettiest cum I'd ever seen in my life. I licked my lips as it trickled out of her pussy, and on my dick, giving me more lubrication.

"Uh-huh. Your lil' chocolate ass been waiting on this, huh?"

She nodded her head up and down fast, while biting her bottom lip. I grabbed her ankles and spread her legs out as far they could go, and started thrusting inside of her ass at a steady pace.

"Daddyyy, oh my Godddd! It feeellll … I can't eevvveenn thhiinkk. Fuck!"

I looked down at her pussy, and I could see her muscles clenching. She was having another orgasm. I looked up in her eyes, and her eyes were halfway open. I grabbed the vibrator that I sat next to her, turned it on, and placed it on her engorged clit.

"Daddy, pllleeassee!" she cried out in pleasure.

"Fuck! This feels so fucking good, Kambridge LeeAnn Lewis-Bailey. I swear to fucking God, a nigga finna marry your sexy ass. Fuck! You mine. Fuck! Baby! You wanna marry a nigga? You wanna be Mrs.

Bailey for real?" I asked, and I was dead ass serious.

She was fucking with my head something serious.

"Dadddy, yess. I wanna marry you … Ahhh, oh my God!"

I let her other ankle go, and she kept her legs spread wide open.

"Good girl. Keep them legs open. Let Daddy see that pretty pussy while he hit this ass," I whispered to her.

I pushed my middle and ring finger inside of her pussy, tapping the G-spot just like she liked. I leaned over and placed a sloppy kiss on her lips, and she started shaking like she was having a seizure, between my dick in her ass, the vibrator on her clit, my fingers in her pussy, and my lips on hers, playing with her tongue.

"DADDDDDYYYYYY! AHHHH FUCK! I HATE YOU, YOU RED FUCKING BASTARRDDD YOU!!!!" she screamed against my lips as she squirted all over us both, but I didn't let up. I wanted to take every ounce of energy she had in her body.

"YOU NEED TO CUMMM, YOU RED BASTARDD! AHHH!" she screamed as she squirted again while fucking me back, and clenching her ass at the same time, making me cum instantly.

One by one, I emptied her holes. She leaned over and laid on the counter. Not even two minutes later, she was knocked out. I picked her up and took her upstairs to bathe us both so we could take an afternoon nap.

Kam

*J*ust like that, I was Mrs. Phoenix Allen Bailey. People may call me crazy, but this man was the love of my life. I knew my dad had ill intentions for me being with him, but I had to thank him for opening my eyes to see what real love is. See, this morning, I thought that Phoenix was joking when he said that he wanted to marry me, but he wasn't. I mean sex makes you say some crazy ass shit, but damn, this nigga was serious. Can we talk about this morning? Phoenix had my fucking legs spread out on the kitchen counter, and was tearing my ass up. Literally. I knew I loved anal sex, but he made me fall in love with it. The vibrator on my clit while pushing his fingers inside of me, made me squirt so hard. I ain't even know I could squirt that much or that long. Us getting married happened fast, but I ain't care.

After we fucked on the kitchen counter, he bathed me then put me in the bed, and I swear that was some of the best sleep that I had ever had in my fucking life. It felt like I had been sleep on a million cotton balls. When I finally woke up, Phoenix was standing in the mirror, messing with his hair. He had on a white linen suit with no shirt. His hard ass tatted up body was on full display.

"Well, you're awake, sleepy head. Seems like you really needed that sleep. I been staring at you for a couple of hours now. You look really beautiful when you are sleeping," he said and smiled.

"You are so creepy, daddy. You know that?" I sleepily said.

I tried to get out of bed, but it felt like my body had been ran over by a garbage truck, so I laid back down. This is how I felt after our first time having sex. It was like he took all the energy that I had in my body. He came over and helped me up out the bed. Laid out on the desk was a white maxi dress and a halo of flowers.

"What's this?" I asked.

"I'm marrying you today. Fuck that. I don't care about the time. You are right for me, and I don't want to spend another second without you having my last name. I went and picked all this up while your ass was knocked out. I mean, if you want to say no, then you can," he said.

The tears started forming in my eyes, and then slowly fell down my face. Of course, I wanted to be his wife. Why would I say no to a man who had shown me more love in just a few short months, than my dad had shown me all my life, and Connor had shown me in the ten years we were together?

"Baby, you can say no! I promise you that I won't be mad," he said. "I won't leave you alone because of it. I can understand if you want to take things slower," he said, wiping my tears away.

"I'm sorry. I'm just overwhelmed. I never knew that anyone would want to marry me. You make me so happy, Phoenix. I have never felt anything like this in my life. Oh my God! Yes, I will marry you. We can get rings later if you want. I don't want you to have to spend none of the money that you have saved up for the building."

"Nah, baby! I got that taken care of. It's not much, but I hope you like it."

He got on one knee, and opened the small black box. It was the cutest ring that I had ever seen. It was a rose gold princess cut diamond ring. It was so shiny, and it was probably two karats.

"Kam, listen. I know you deserve better than this, but I promise if you stick with me, I will get you something bigger and better than⌧"

"Sshhhhhh." I placed a finger on his lips. "Rings are materialistic. I don't care about no ring as long as I get to spend the rest of my life with the man who makes me the happiest woman in the world."

He placed the ring on my finger. I could barely get dressed because I was staring at my ring. If I had social media, I would be showing my ring off to the world.

"Are you going to wear a ring?" I asked him.

"You wouldn't care if I didn't?" he replied.

I shrugged my shoulders. "I don't know. Rings don't mean shit, if we are being honest, because men cheat with them, and they cheat without them. Women too, before you say something slick," I chuckled.

When I finally got dressed, Mr. Parker took us to the St. Maarten Courthouse, where Phoenix and I became husband and wife. So, yeah, that's how that happened. Now, we were sitting in our cabana on the beach, throwing back several drinks, celebrating our union. Phoenix kept taking pictures of our wedding rings. This nigga had bought himself a ring too, and had it in his pocket. During our ceremony, he put on my wedding band, then pulled his band out his pocket, and put it on his own hand. I chuckled when he did that. Nothing about our ceremony was orthodox, but I wouldn't change it for the world.

"Can you believe that we got married, baby?" he laughed. "The way that ass clenched down on my dick, I knew then that I was going to marry your chocolate ass. Aye, I don't want you to think that I'm crazy or whatever, but we ain't never getting a divorce. You belong to me," he said while looking me directly in my eyes.

"So, when are we going to tell our parents that we are married? I'm not so sure I want to tell my parents just yet. They are probably going to put me out once I tell them," I expressed.

"Chill, girl. We are going to tell them when the time is right, I promise you that. If your daddy lays a hand on you, I'm going to kill him. As your husband, it is my duty to protect and provide for you. So when we get back to the States, I want you to start looking for us a spot together. Don't have to be big, and it don't have to be small. I just want us to be comfortable," he said and placed his hand on my stomach.

He swore up and down that I was going to be pregnant once we left St. Maarten, and I probably was because I checked my period tracker, and I was in my fertility window. At least I'd be married when I give birth. That's one thing that I always wanted.

"Babe, we are getting ready to try and open a business. We can continue our living arrangements for now until we get Rich Cutz off the ground."

"Damn, baby, I just want to be able to be under the same roof with you every fucking night, and kissing all over your pretty ass. Dipping my tongue and my dick in that sweet nectar of yours," he said, nuzzling in my neck.

"In due time, baby, in due time," I said as I snapped a photo of him nuzzling in my neck. We had taken so many pictures and videos that I was probably going to have to buy new storage.

"I'm about to go get us something to eat and some more to drink. Do you want anything specifically?"

"Whatever you bring back is fine, Mr. Bailey."

"Okay, I'll be right back, Mrs. Bailey. Damn that sounds good," he said before he stepped through the curtain of the cabana.

I watched Phoenix walk away, and I couldn't help but to think that I was so lucky to have a man like him, who would always have my best interest at heart. The way he makes me blush whenever he gives me a compliment. The way he takes care of my body. Ever since he bust my cherry, we been having good ass sex, and I swear I hoped sex was not clouding our judgement here.

While Phoenix was out getting our food, I had made a group chat, and sent a picture of our marriage license and wedding rings to Kade, Kalena, and Shelly. Not even two seconds after putting my phone down, the messages started coming in like crazy.

Kade: *WTF!!!!!!!! Kambridge what the fuck did you do? You better be fucking playing. I know you ain't get married to that nigga. You trippin' trippin'. Are you pregnant or something? Mane, I'm so mad with you right now. Where the fuck that nigga at? I'm about to call him.*

Kalena: *Shut up, Kade. Big Sissy, I am sooo happy for you. I love Phoenix for you, and he loves you back. You are the smartest person I know, and I know that you made the right decision. I can't wait until you get pregnant and have a baby.*

Shelly: *Stfu Kade. Kam is grown, and she loves that man. He loves her. That's what people in love do.*

Shelly: *That's a nice ass ring, Kambridge. I'm so happy for you, and you are the most deserving person I know. I'm with Kalena. I want a niece!*

Kalena: *Are we supposed to keep this a secret? Mom and dad is sitting here looking at me because I screamed when I saw that ring.*

Me: *Yes! Please keep it a secret. I'm going to tell them soon.*

Me: *Y'all. It just feels so right. I'm so in love with him. Kade, I swear he treats me just like you always treat me. He loves me and treats me with nothing but respect. He loves me for who I am and thinks I'm the most beautiful person in the world with or without make-up unlike... you know. I can truly be myself when I am with him. Our chemistry is off the charts. I just can't explain it, but he is the one for me.*

Kade: *I'm on the phone with him now, and he is telling me how much he loves you. He is telling me that he can't put a time on love. He pretty much saying what you just text: he can't explain it, but he knows it's real. He is promising me that he will never hurt you intentionally, and that he promises to protect and provide for you. I can't argue with that, Kambridge. Just know that I am always going to be here for you, if you need me. Mom and dad is going to be PISSSSEEEDDD when they find out.*

Me: *Thank you for being supportive, Kade. I probably won't tell Mom and Dad until I am moving out of their house and into a place with my husband. That sounds so good... my husband. I'll talk to y'all later.*

I put my phone down just as Phoenix was walking up with his earbuds in his ear, carrying our food on a tray.

"Yeah, like I said. I vow to love and protect this woman for the rest of my life. Now let me get back to my wife, nigga. We can talk face to face when we touch down. Peace," he said, and pulled his earbuds out his ear.

I knew that he was on the phone with Kade.

"Baby, after we finish eating, I have so much planned for us to do. We are going to snorkel, parasail, and jet ski. After that, we are going to come back to the house, and make love for the first time as husband and wife. How do you feel about that?" I asked.

"This your world, baby. I'm just living in it."

I laughed so hard because I remembered he said that all the time when we were first getting to know each other. While we were eating, we both kept stealing glances at each other, and smiling like two teenagers who were flirting with each other. After we finished eating, we gathered our things to head down to the jet skis. Luckily, I had on my swimsuit under my maxi dress, and Phoenix had on some swim shorts under his pants.

"I feel bad that I didn't ask you this before, but can you swim?" I asked him.

"Yes, wife. I can swim. Did you forget that I have a pool? I need to be asking you that, since you don't have a pool at that big ass house," he replied.

"Yeah, my dad put us in swim lessons when I was younger."

"Prep-school ass. Everybody I know, dad pushed them in the pool and watched them struggle for a minute, and that's how they learned how to swim," he laughed.

"Actually, that is very traumatizing for a child. I'm surprised you still learned how to swim, and if you think for one second that's how you're going to teach our children how to swim, then you need to rethink that thought," I snapped before I knew it.

"How about this? You raise the girls, and I raise the boys. You focus on doing pigtails, and painting toenails, and let me focus on hunting and the haircuts," he smirked.

Laughing, I replied, "That is not how parenting works, you idiot. WE both parent both kids, but you know what? As long as daddy slides that black card over whenever we go get our hair done and toes painted, we will gladly stay out of the men's way."

"You ain't gon' start my daughter with that black card shit, because although my princess is going to have me wrapped around her finger, I'm still going to know how to say 'no' to her. On second thought, if she looks anything like her chocolate ass mama, she won't hear no often. Kam, you don't know what your eyes do to me, man, especially when I'm hitting that pussy in the right spot. They be half-open and rolling in the back of your head. Your eyes tell it all, baby."

"Oh my God!" He had me blushing.

For the next several hours, we did all the watersports that the beach had to offer, and my body was so tired after we were a thousand feet in the air, parasailing. I wasn't as scared as Phoenix ass was. He kept saying that he wasn't scared, but I knew that he was. He said that all he was picturing was a shark jumping out the water, and catching us in his mouth. I almost passed out from laughing so hard.

We were walking along the beach as the sun was setting, and the pink and orange colors was so beautiful. I took my Nikon out my bag and started taking pictures of it. I instructed Phoenix to stand in the water, with his back towards me. He had put on a shirt with my logo on the back, so I could post it on my business page on Facebook. The sunset made the picture perfect. He turned around, and I took another one, catching him off guard. It was the best picture too.

Strolling up to the house, he opened the door for me, and the minute I stepped inside, my mouth dropped. There were dozens and dozens of white and red roses everywhere. There were petals torn off and on the floor. There were little tea lights lined up in the hallway which was the only light in the house. Phoenix set our bags down at the door and led me to the master bedroom. There were more rose petals on top of the bed cover, and more tea lights in the room.

He turned around to me, lifted my chin up, and traced my lips with the tip of his tongue, then tongued me down for several minutes. He slowly undressed me, and led me to the bathroom. The garden tub was full of water, and rose petals. I could tell that he had a put a bath bomb in the water because it was light pink. After he helped me in the tub, he left out the bathroom, and I heard the music come through the speakers. Moments later, he came back with champagne flutes, and a bottle of champagne. He poured us some glasses. He handed me mine, sat on the sink, and watched me.

"When did you plan all of this?" I asked.

"Well, we are celebrating our honeymoon. So this came as a part of a package, but you know I paid a little extra for the rose petals and tea lights."

"Are you getting in with me?"

He shook his head at me and then pulled his medicine out his pocket. His medicine being his weed. I had only seen him roll up some weed once, and I was intrigued by it, but he ain't let me smoke.

"You okay? Why are you smoking?"

"We are on vacation, and this is for the both of us. You finna hit this, and the sex is going to be on ten. Kam, I'm about to blow your mind, girl," he said as if he could blow my mind any more than he already had.

He lit it and brought it over to me. He instructed me on how to pull and inhale. I did it the first time, and I almost coughed up a lung.

"Slower this time, Kambridge Bailey," he laughed.

I did it, and this time it felt better. We kept passing it back and forth until it was gone. He rolled another one, but he said that it was for after we had sex. After soaking my body for another twenty minutes, we both got in the shower, to wash and rinse. After we got out, he wrapped a towel around me and then wrapped a towel around his waist. He dried me off and then laid me down on the bed. He gave me a full body massage. My body was so mellow from smoking weed, and between that feeling and my husband massaging me, sleep was almost taking me over. When he was done, he grabbed my phone and set it up to record us.

"This is for you when I'm not around," he said.

I was already on my stomach, so he started placing soft kisses all over my back, and then down to my ass cheeks. He bit both of them hard as fuck, making me yelp out in pain. Phoenix then spread my ass cheeks, and then licked his wet tongue up and down the crack of my ass. He then rested his arms on the top of my ass and dove in my pussy.

"Fuck! I love eating this pussy," he groaned inside of my pussy.

He stood up and his towel fell. He raised my bottom half up and slid under me. He slid me up on his face to where his dick was in my face. I started sucking on it while he was devouring my pussy. The way Phoenix's tongue was circling my clit, I couldn't concentrate, so his dick was just sitting in my mouth.

"Kam ... My dick is not a thermometer. Suck that shit!" he commanded, and smacked my ass.

While I was sucking his dick and playing with his balls at the same time, I thought about that spot that Shelly told me to lick to watch him go crazy. I lifted his balls up, and started licking on that spot between his asshole and his balls.

Kammmmbriddgee," he moaned as his body shuddered under me.

I caught a glimpse of his toes, and they were damn near throwing up the gang signs. I was massaging his balls while stroking his dick, and licking on that spot at the same time. I had to get him back from the way he did me this morning. Licking it wasn't enough; I needed his soul, so I started sucking and nibbling on it.

"Kambridgeeee!" His voice even went up an octave. "Fucckkkk! Damn it, woman!"

His dick was pulsating in my hand, and then he exploded. The cum was coming down the sides like lava, so I put his dick in my mouth to catch the rest of it. After I stroked all his cum out of him, he pushed me forward.

"Sit on that big mothafucka, Kam. Let me see if you can ride it in reverse cowgirl," he said.

 I positioned myself comfortably and slid down on his dick. He guided me with his hands until I found my own rhythm. I leaned over and latched on to his ankles, making my little ass clap while I rode him.

"Damn, mama! Shit, slow down before I cum again!"

He spread my ass cheeks with one hand, and I felt something cold entering my ass.

"Damn, what's that, baby?"

"I put the butt plug in the fridge before we left."

Once it was comfortably in my ass, he instructed me to put my feet in between his legs. Once I did that, he started raising his back up off the bed a little at a time. Somehow, we both ended up on our knees, with his dick never falling out of my pussy. This nigga's skills in the bedroom would never get old to me. He had one arm around my waist and his hand around my neck. He started slow stroking me, and when he did that, his pelvis was putting pressure on the butt plug, giving me more pleasure than I could ever imagine.

"Fuckk, daddy! This dick is so fucking good. How you learn to fuck this fucking good?" I moaned out.

"Kamm, I'm so happy I made you my wife," he whispered in my ear. "I promise to love you forever. I promise to protect you from anything and anybody. Fuck. You belong to me, Kambridge Leeann Bailey. You know that, right?"

"I'm about to cum, daddy!" I cried out.

"Daddy knows! I feel it, baby."

He gave me a long lick down my back, as far as he could without his dick falling out of me. He was kissing all over my scars and even licking them. He sunk his teeth into my shoulder, while he continued to stroke me. The hand that was around my waist went between my legs, and he started playing with my clit.

"Daddy, you feel so fucking good to me. I need you to fuck me! Hard!" I moaned.

He pushed me face first into the bed, and started beating my pussy up. I kept trying to push him back, but he kept smacking my hands away.

"This what you wanted. You better take this fucking, dick! You my bitch, huh?" he growled.

"Yesssss!"

"SAY IT! SAY IT, KAM BAILEY! SCREAM IT!

"DADDY! I'M YOUR BITTTCCHHH! OH MY GODD!"

I was cumming all over his dick, and he kept going. I was losing my mind, and moments later, he sprayed my walls with his warm cum. He pulled out of me and laid next to me, trying to catch his breath.

"Who the fuck told you about that spot that you were sucking and licking on? You fucked my head all the way up with that. Kam, I swear to God, if you put your mouth on another nigga, I'll probably kill you," he said.

I started laughing at him. He sat up and got the blunt off the nightstand and lit it. He got up to turn the camera off. He plopped down next to me, but I was stuck on my stomach. I couldn't move from that beatdown he had just given me, plus, the butt plug was still in my ass.

"Oh, my bad." He laughed and took the butt plug out my ass.

Once he took it out, I rolled over on my back. He put pillows under our head so we could finish smoking.

"Kam, I ain't never letting you go," he said.

I ain't reply, but we continued to pass the blunt back and forth until we finished it. We got under the covers and fell asleep in each other's arms.

Tracey Lewis

I bit down on my bottom lip, trying to muffle my moans, as I watched Malice pound into my daughter's pussy like his life depended on it. I have watched this video like five times already … this morning. She hadn't texted me since she'd been on vacation, so after Kalena's outburst at the dinner table, I wanted to know what was going on, but she didn't tell me. I let it go until this morning, after I hacked into Kambridge's iCloud, so I was seeing everything. I read over all her messages, and I saw that her and Malice had got married yesterday, and that's what Kalena was so fucking happy about. I ventured over into her pictures, and there were so many of them. Malice looked genuinely happy with my daughter, and I couldn't help but to be jealous. What did I venture into the videos for? I watched Malice and my daughter fuck. I kept watching it over and over again. I couldn't stop watching it. Every time I watched it, I bust a nut of my own, just thinking about how he would fuck me until I could barely walk. That nigga was worth every bit of that three thousand dollars I paid him every time we fucked, and my fucking daughter was getting all that shit for FREE!

See, Kambridge wasn't supposed to be born. Even though she wasn't supposed to be born, doesn't mean that I didn't love her any less than my other kids. See, around the time that Kambridge was conceived, Kason and I were barely fucking. He was putting his all into his stupid campaign to be the judge, leaving me alone to myself to deal with Kade's ass. I loved my son more than anything, but I was needing a break.

One day, I was in the grocery store, and I ran into Trent Wilson, or Big Will. Big Will was fine as hell. He was super dark skinned, with long thick hair that he had in two big braids. He looked like he could be an Indian. I was so drawn to him that I couldn't even say a word to him, but he approached me. We exchanged numbers and met up later that week when I was supposed to be at work. I fucked him the first time we spent time together, and continued to fuck him every other day, until I ended up pregnant five months later. That dick was so good. I was going to get rid of the baby, but everyone knew us because my husband's face was on every TV in Chicago. There was no way I could get in and out of an abortion clinic with no one noticing who I was and selling my fucking medical records to the media. I thought about taking a lot of pills, but that would have made my husband look bad, so I was fucked either way.

When Trent found out about me being pregnant, he was so excited, but I told him that it was my husband's baby; he didn't believe me for one second. I had to promise him that I would let him be in the baby's life for him not to go to the media about him being my child's dad. I promised him because my back was against the wall. The day Kam was born, Trent showed up to the hospital with balloons and a card. Trent and Kason had words, and Trent got put out the hospital. Not even a month later, Kason locked Trent up for the rest of his life. I knew it was my fault. If I can remember correctly, I sent Trent a picture of Kambridge on her first birthday, and that was the last time I had any type of contact with him.

Trent was really starting to feel me, but of course, we couldn't take it that far. I wasn't leaving my husband, and he knew it. He always talked about Korupt, and that's why when Malice mentioned Korupt being his daddy, I damn near shit myself. That was one of the legit reasons why I didn't want Kam talking to Malice. So many secrets could come out that we had buried for so long. I was so happy that Kam looked like my mom. Well, she had Trent's long, thick hair, his rich chocolate skin, and his big ass eyes. Everything else came from my mom. I guess I can thank God for that.

After Kason locked Trent up for the rest of his life, Kason changed … for the worst. The first time he started hitting Kam, she was a year old. I don't even know what she did, but she had walked in my room crying. Her bottom was so red, and I told Kason that he was out of line for hitting her, but that's all I did. I begged him for a divorce, but he told me no and that he would kill me and get away with it. I used to take my baby girl to the doctor with bruises all over her body, but Kason slid the doctor thousands of dollars to not call CPS. He told me that he forgave me for cheating on him, but over the years, the beatings got worse. The first time he beat her bloody was after a recital. She missed one note while playing her violin, and he brought her home and beat her down. I tried to stop him, but he pushed me away. He didn't stop until she passed out. He told me that I'd better take her to her room and nurse her wounds because she wasn't going to the hospital.

See, … I was stuck between a rock and a hard place because I wanted to leave. I needed to leave to protect my kids. I should have left to protect my daughter from him, but what was the point of me leaving if Kason would have killed me and Kam would have gone to him anyway. It got to the point when I heard her screams, I would just turn the TV up to drown it out. Who was I going to tell? The police? Kason is the police. Kason is the judge and the jury. Kason is the devil. Kason is the Grim Reaper. Kason has more secrets than the average person, and he thought no one knew.

The knock on my door made me close out the sex tape of Malice and my daughter.

"It's open," I said.

Cara pushed the door open and walked in. She was looking crazy in the face, and I prayed that she didn't have any work that she needed me to do. I only had one boss and that was Cara. She was also the woman who gave me Malice's information.

"Um, I have a question. It's not work related. Do you have a minute?" she asked.

"Yes, I'm not busy."

"When was your last appointment with Malice? He just cancelled all my appointments with no explanation, and it's bothering me. Did he cancel your appointments as well?"

I nodded my head. I wasn't about to put all my business out there in the streets like that. I was just as pissed as she was.

"Damn, I wonder what happened. I hadn't had any of that monster in a month and I'm losing it. I'm damn near about to stalk his young ass," she laughed. "That's all I wanted. Let me know if he opens up his schedule again."

When she left out of my office, an idea popped up in my head. I sent Cara an email to let her know that I was getting ready to leave for the day. In the parking lot, I pulled my phone out and went back into Kam's iCloud and went back in her videos. I saw that a few more videos had been added. The first video was Kam sucking his long, thick dick. She was making it disappear in her fucking throat, and Malice was in the background yelping like she was sucking his voice out of him.

"Fuuuckkk, mama! Fuck, mama! I'm in love with youuu. Fuck! Catch daddy's nut," he growled at her.

She held her head back like a fucking puppy dog while Malice shot his nut in her mouth. The jealousy that soared through my body made my eyes water. I clicked on the second video, and Malice was eating Kam's pussy. She was shaking so bad that she could barely record him.

"I know the feeling," I said to myself.

His long, thick tongue was penetrating her pussy, and I could see that he was sucking the nut right out of her. He was swallowing it like it was orange juice. I shouldn't have been watching my daughter's sex tapes, but she was having sex with the man that I was supposed to be having sex with. The third video was Malice fucking Kam doggy style. He had a butt plug in her ass, and he was tearing her ass up. I turned the video off and threw my phone in the passenger seat.

"That was supposed to be me! Ahhh!" I said, and banged my forehead against my steering wheel.

I pulled out of the parking lot, and sped to the direction of Kam's store. Luckily, the whole block's power was out from the storm last night, so all the businesses were closed. I pulled my car around back. I got my bat out the trunk of my car, and got my spare pair of gloves out of my glove compartment. I picked her lock to the back door, and the first thing I did was tear the cameras out the wall. Even though there was no power, you never knew how cameras worked these days. They could still be recording.

I went in her back room, and started fucking up everything. I busted up everything. I worked my way from the back room to the front. I knocked down all the mugs. Everything that I could break up, that's what I did. I got some of her spray paint that she kept on her bottom shelf, and sprayed everything.

Two hours after destroying Kam's store, I chuckled at my handiwork. I knew I was wrong for doing this, but she was fucking my man. She even married the man that I was going to leave my husband for. Once he realized that Kam couldn't do anything for him, he would run back to me. I had way more money than Kam. He wouldn't ever have to fuck for money again. I could take care of both of us. I just needed him to understand that.

I left Kam's store and sped home. I got rid of all the spray paint cans in a McDonald's trashcan twenty miles away from the store along the way home. When I made it home, no one was there, so I went into our shed, got some of this special solution, and went in the house to wipe down Kam's room well.

See, people may have thought I was a bad parent, but I didn't think I was. She just took what was mine, and I have to get it back. I would do anything I had to do to get it back. That's all.

Judge Kason Lewis

essed in all black, I was in my warehouse, an hour away from Chicago. These mothafuckas were trying my fucking patience.

"WHY AIN'T THESE NIGGAS DEAD!" I roared to my crew.

"Sir, Grim Reaper, sir, may I speak?"

"If you ain't about to answer my mothafuckin' question, then hell naw you can't speak," I shot at Chow.

Chow cleared his throat and stood up before he started speaking.

"Grim Reaper, they are hard to get to. Their security is airtight just like yours. Before we can get one shot off at them niggas, they are already letting off twenty shots. None of them go nowhere by themselves. Since you locked up Frank, they shut everything down. We hit two of their warehouses in one week, and there was no drugs or money in there. Our crew is not strong enough. It seems like everybody in Chicago is already pushing weight for Mayhem and his daddy. We even went to the neighboring states, and everybody already collaborating with Korupt," Chow spoke and then sat down.

I looked around the room at the thirty young guys that I had in attendance. It seemed like they were all agreeing with Chow because they were shaking their heads. I waved my hand to end the meeting, and they all filed out of the room, including my security team.

Yeah, call me a hypocrite, I don't care. People say money is the root of all evil, but to me, it's not. It's the power. I wanted all the power. Knowing that I had people's fate in my hands, damn near made my dick hard. Listening to people grovel at my feet made my heart swell. I wanted all the power including the streets, but it'd been hard trying to take the streets from Korupt. That nigga had more power than I thought he did. It was hard to get to him.

"Shaw, go make sure all of them are gone," I ordered him. "Make sure my security stays outside as well."

When he got up and left, I lit my cigar. I needed to relax my nerves a little bit. Shaw came back in ten minutes to let me know that they were all gone. I told him to follow me to another room in the back of the warehouse. I hit the light switch, pressed a code into the keypad next to a light switch, and an automated door popped open from the roof. I stood on my tiptoes, pulled the light fixture, and pulled it all the way down. The wooden ladder slid down, and Shaw followed me up the stairs and got the shock of his lifetime. I hadn't told anyone about this to this day.

"Judge," he whispered. "Is this real?"

"Yeah, I been had this for almost thirty years. It's worth millions. The only thing I have used with this money is to pay for my schooling. I actually stole this from Korupt when he went to jail," I admitted.

"Quick question, and it may be a stupid question, considering the fact that we are standing in a room full of his gold. Is there a specific reason why you don't want to work with Korupt or☒"

"I just don't want to work with him. We have had our fair share of problems, and it wouldn't work anyway," I replied. "Shaw, you are the first person I ever told this to, so hopefully, I won't hear of this again. Loose lips sink ships is something to remember."

I went over and pulled a gold bar off the top of one stack and put it in my bag. I know I told Shaw about it, but I was going to come back later tonight and move all this shit again. In my line of work, it was hard to trust anyone, even Shaw. He'd been working with me for the last decade, but you never knew what people would do for money. I'm the perfect example of that.

Shaw and I rode together, so after I locked up the building, we headed back to the city with my security in tow. The ride was quiet until he said what I been wanting to hear for months.

"Well, Malice told Kambridge that his dad was a drug dealer amongst other things. I'm not sure if you would want to hear it, though."

"Yeah, I want to hear it."

He plugged his phone into my radio, and it came alive. That little nigga was telling my daughter how his dad and brother were drug dealers. He was telling her how his dad wanted him to get in the family business, but he didn't want to. He kept going on and on, and then told my baby girl that the only difference between me and Korupt, is that I'm abusive. I told Shaw to turn it off.

"Sir, I don't mean to pry⊠"

"Well, don't!" I snarled.

"I think there is more on this tape that you should⊠"

"Shut the fuck up!"

The beauty of being a powerful man, is that you can get whatever it is that you want. When Kam told me that she was going on vacation, I got a mini recorder and placed it in her bag. She would have never noticed it. She ain't have to tell me that she was going with that nigga because I knew. I ain't crazy. After everything that I heard on the tape, the only thing that truly bothered me was that nigga talking about his uncle Trent. The LAST thing I needed was Kambridge up in that jailhouse, visiting that nigga with Malice. Fuck! I swear, if it ain't one thing it's another.

Back in the day, Korupt was a cool ass nigga. We both ran in two different circles though. To be fair, Korupt helped a lot of people, including me, unless you were on his bad side. He was the reason that I could keep my sneakers for my senior year. I didn't have any dreams of being a corner boy or any of that shit, but once I saw how Korupt and Big Will were getting money, I wanted in. I needed to help my parents pay some of their bills and to keep some lunch money in my pocket. That's where my obsession with power came from, so I could partially blame him for the way I am now.

Honestly, I ain't want to be a judge. Hell, I ain't even know what I wanted to do when I was a senior in high school. I didn't plan on going to college, because I couldn't afford it. I was just going with the flow until one day I was watching this TV show where the judge was an undercover drug dealer. He was taking million-dollar bribes and locking people up all in the same day. That's when I told Korupt that I needed extra money to rob that store. I dropped his gun on purpose. Why? I had walked in his house one week earlier, and I overheard him talking about the gold, to his now wife, Angela. Genius. I know right.

Stealing his gold was easy. The minute he went to jail, he told me about the gold and then told me that I was the only person who knew where it was. So when he told me that he didn't tell Trent, I put a plan into motion. Moved the gold to a secret location. Paid for college and law school. Moved my parents out the hood. I was living the dream … until Korupt got out. That nigga was killing friends from college … friends from high school trying to find that shit, but he got nothing, but when he killed my parents … that was a different type of hurt for me. Nigga even had the nerve to show up to my parents' funeral like I didn't know he was the one behind all the shit. After that shit, I took the bar exam and started locking his crew up left and right. Starting with the one who had cost me the most pain in my life … Trent.

After I dropped Shaw off, I turned a few corners and made my way back out to my warehouse to move the gold … again. I smiled to myself when I thought about the recording that Shaw let me hear. Malice had finally opened up to my baby girl, and now it was time to dead the relationship so I could put all these niggas in jail and truly take over the city. I was only going to give her one chance to end the relationship … then I was going to have to my foot down ... literally. As bad as it pained my insides, I hadn't put my hands on her for the past few weeks. I needed her to feel like she won, but little do she know … that was all a part of my plan.

Korupt

*K*ason can't be as smart as I thought he was if he thought that he could assemble a crew in my city, and I not find out about it. Drugs ain't even his cup of tea, but he trying to start a fucking crew. I laughed a hearty laugh when Mayhem told me that shit. See, after Mayhem's guy, Frank got knocked, I shut down everything. Well mostly everything. The most loyal customers knew to go to the back door of some of the bodegas to get served. The taxi company was shut down for now, but I kept my workers' pockets laced so they can feed their families. I'm not that type of a guy.

"Is there anything else you need to tell me," I asked Chow who was standing in front of me.

"Nah, boss. He dismissed us after I told him that you were too powerful. I told him that ain't nobody trying to work with him. He trying to take you down man," he said.

"Tell me something I don't know. If I need you again, Mayhem will be in contact with you. Thank you for your information," I said, and slid him five thousand dollars.

Once Chow was out of my office, I laughed a hearty laugh.

"Who that nigga think he is? Talking about call him 'Grim Reaper'. That nigga don't know shit about killing nobody. He can't even rob a damn store good. How he gon' kill anybody?" I said to Mayhem.

I had sent a few people to the warehouse Chow said they were last night, and I was waiting on the phone call, which should be coming in momentarily, because I sent them, as soon as he told me the location.

"Your brother still in another country with that bitch?" I asked.

He nodded his head before replying, "Dad, your plan backfired. He really is in love with that girl, and I honestly don't believe that girl knows anything about her dad's past life. That I know for sure. I've talked to her when she's stayed over to the house, and she is a nice girl. They love each other, and there is nothing that you will be able to do about that. Happened fast, but I believe it's real," he said.

"Whatever." I waved him off.

"I'm telling you because she is coming over for dinner when they get back, and I'm telling you to be on your best behavior. If you don't do anything else for Malice, do this for him. He don't ask you for anything."

"Nigga, who are you to be telling me to *be on my best behavior?*" I laughed.

Before he could reply, my phone rang, and I picked it up on the first ring.

"Yeah," I answered.

"There was nothing in there. Went into a room, busted up a keypad, and went into an attic like thing. There was nothing there either. You think that lil' nigga was lying?" Theo said into the phone.

"Nah, I believe him. It's all good though," I said and hung up the phone.

"Now, back to you," I said to Mayhem. "When is she coming for dinner, and why?"

"That's what people in relationships do, ... meet each other's parents. Forget all of that, is the Playa's Ball still going to be on since we shut everything down?"

"Son, ain't shit stopping that Playa's Ball. Matter of fact, we need to start prepping for it as soon as possible. Go make some calls to whoever you need to make some calls to so we can pay who we need to pay so that bitch can be fly as fuck!"

My son nodded his head, got up, and left my office. The Playa's Ball was something that the Bailey's hosted every year. This will be the tenth annual Playa's Ball. This is basically a party that brings the city out. They dress in their finest gear, and the dress code is strictly enforced. No tennis shoes, no hats, just gowns and tuxedos. Security is heavy on the outside and the inside, so my people can really be relaxed in the building. They don't have to bring their guns in there while they are chilling with their lady or whoever. Women can get their bills paid, and niggas can get their dick wet for the night. I love to see my people have fun with no violence.

Contrary to popular belief, I really am a good person. I do a lot for the community, including the Playa's Ball. It's completely free to the public. They even eat free. It's like one big gala. You can sit and eat, or you can hit the dance floor. The Playa's Ball is where I found out that Malice was fucking that crazy ass white bitch, Catherine. At the very first Playa's Ball, she showed up and was looking good as hell. She didn't stand out because there were a lot of white people there. Her and Malice weren't even saying anything to each other. I went to one of the back rooms of the building to take a phone call, and the door was cracked. Malice had her pinned against the wall, fucking the shit out of her, and I was rooting for my son because I knew that she was older. I was getting ready to leave the door until I heard her say that he was worth every penny that she paid him. Actually, I was heartbroken to know that my son would rather fuck women for money than to work with me. After that, I had him trailed for a few months and saw that my son was fucking a lot more women for money. I checked his bank account, and that shit was nice, so I couldn't really argue, and he was eighteen, so he was grown.

"Paxton, this came for you in the mail," my beautiful wife, Angela, said, walking in my office and throwing a package on my desk.

The only weaknesses I have in the world are my wife and my kids. That's it. If I lost any one of them, I would probably have a heart attack and die. They were the reason that I breathed and worked as hard as I did. Angela and I been together since way before Mayhem was born. I hadn't always been the perfect man, but she stuck with a nigga until I got my shit together.

"Thank you, mama! You better be ready for this dick tonight," I said to her.

"Only if you are eating this ass," she laughed.

"Girl, anything you want me to do, I'll do it, as long as I'm next to you."

She blushed and walked out the door. *Damn, I really love that woman.* I looked at the box that she had on my desk. I was confused because I hadn't ordered anything. The box didn't even have a return address. I shook the box, but I didn't hear anything. Carefully, I opened the box, and my attitude instantly changed.

In the box was one gold bar with a note attached that said *LOL*. I could feel my blood pressure rising. Kason was really fucking trying me, and I swear to God that I was going to kill that nigga if that was the last thing that I did. I picked up the phone to give him a call down to the courthouse. I had a very secure line, so no one in the courthouse would be able to track the phone call. The phone was answered on the first ring.

"This is Paxton Bailey, is Judge Kason Lewis in?" I spoke through gritted teeth, trying to sound as professional as possible.

"Sure, I can transfer you right now."

I was put on hold for about two minutes before he came on the phone.

"This is Judge Kason Lewis; how may I be of service to you today?" he said in such a chipper voice.

"You listen to me, you thieving ass nigga. You wait until I get close to⊠"

"Mr. Bailey, you wouldn't be threatening a judge over the phone, now would you?" he chuckled.

"Kason, you play a lot of games, but you acting like you ain't got secrets that can put you away for a very long time," I spoke through gritted teeth. "See, I ain't no bitch ass nigga, and you know the only way I handle shit is in the streets … with violence. You keep fucking with me, and everyone is going to know what type of a person you really are. Bring me my shit."

"If I'm not mistaking, I don't owe you anything. Everything that has happened to you is because of you … not me."

"You know, Mr. Grim … In a few days, I will be having company. The company of a very beautiful young woman. Kambridge, is it?"

"Who you call me?" he spat into the phone.

"Do I need to remind you that this is my city? Nothing gets by me."

"Except what's in that box … That got by you. You are acting like I give a fuck. She ain't my daughter anyway." He tried to sound hard on the phone, knowing he wouldn't bust a grape in Welch's backyard.

I chuckled before I replied, "You know, Kason, if I thought for one second that you actually felt that way about Kambridge, I would go shoot a crow and eat it. Well, on second thought, a man who is abusing anyone, doesn't love them. Kason, if I haven't learned anything about you over the years, I have learned that you hate to lose. If you don't stop fucking with me, you are going to lose … a lot. Good day," I said and hung up the phone.

Kason was really trying my patience. He was going to end up making me kill him and not even get my damn gold.

Kam

$\mathcal{T}$he vacation was everything that I never knew I needed, until my feet were playing in the sand for five days in a row. That let me know that I needed to vacation more often than I do instead of the once or twice a year that I did. I didn't come on vacation to get married, but we did it, and I didn't feel like I'd made a bad decision. Even though my husband was mad at me, he still didn't let me carry anything, as he had all the luggage rolling through the airport. For the life of me, I didn't know where these mood swings and dizzy spells were coming from, but they were coming frequently. It's like I would get a headache, and then my whole mood would change. I'd get dizzy, and I'd wig out. Hubby was telling me that I needed to go get it checked out because he would hate to have to put hands on me. I laughed at him because that nigga was just a gentle giant. He would never put his hands on me.

This morning, I woke up with a headache, and all my hubby was trying to do was serve me breakfast in bed, and I knocked the tray out of his hand. I started yelling at him for no reason. He hadn't talked to me since then. I laid in the bed while he silently packed the rest of our things. In the car on the way to the airport, I was feeling better, and I tried to talk to him, but he didn't say a word. We rode on the airplane in silence, and now we were in the car in silence.

"Phoenix, I'm sorry. I don't know what's going on with me, but

I'm going to the doctor to get checked out. I have never felt the way that I'm feeling. Can you please forgive me, or at least say something? Do you want an annulment? If you do, I will understand," I solemnly said.

"Kambridge, I don't know if you heard what I said back in St. Maarten, but I told you that I ain't never letting you go. We are going to get you checked out to see what is going on with you, okay? Please don't go to that *divorce* shit every time we get into a fight. That's what people in relationships do, … fight. If they don't fight, …then they shit fake as fuck, or they don't love each other anymore. I love you, Kam, and as long as we both in love with each other, we can make this shit work," he said, and I could literally feel my heart swelling up with joy.

"Damn, how the fuck I end up with you for a husband?" I swooned and then kissed his hand.

"Nah, the real question is how did I end up with you as a wife. So, whose parents are we going to tell first that we are married?"

"We are definitely going to tell your parents first. It seems like they will probably be more understanding than my parents. I'm excited to even meet them. I wonder what Mr. Korupt is like," I said and looked out the window.

"He's different than most, I can tell you that." He laughed as he pulled my car into his driveway.

"Um, I just want to let you know that I am not going to be wearing my ring around my parents. I don't want you to think that I would be taking it off just for the fuck of it. I just don't want them asking questions. Let's just get a chain and wear it around our necks for the time being," I offered.

"I have two small chains in the house," he said.

After we grabbed the chains, he placed it around my neck and then kissed the ring. He promised me that he was going to be with me forever, and I believed him. He walked me back out to the car and kissed me so passionately that I started stroking his dick, but he moved back, making me roll my eyes.

"Don't start nothing you can't finish, lil' woman. I'll have you out here screaming my name." He groaned as I kept stroking his dick.

Looking up at my suntanned husband, while he bit his lip, turned me on so much. I moved my hand inside of his pants, and gripped his now fully hard dick. I stuck my other hand in his pants, and started playing with his nuts at the same time.

"Kam, baby." He let out a low groan. "Keep doing it just like that, mama."

"I wanna see it, baby. Pull your pants down," I commanded.

He pulled his pants down enough until his balls were out. I kept stroking, and he latched on to my shoulders, and I knew that he was getting ready to cum. His nut shot out and covered the sides of his dick.

"I love watching that cum come out that dick, daddy! It's so fucking sexy," I said as I stroked the rest of it out.

The garage came open, and we saw Mayhem pulling in, so he hurriedly pulled his pants up. He walked to the back of my car and got his luggage out the trunk. He kissed me one more time before he opened the door for me. I grabbed a towel to wipe my hands off, and he shut the door for me. I let the window down to stare at him.

"You so fine," I said.

"Your lil' ass so beautiful, mama!" he replied.

"Are we going to meet at the bank tomorrow after lunch, or what?" I asked him.

"Yes! Yes, we are. I'm also going to put you on my bank account as well, wife! Damn! That sounds good," he said.

I let the window up and backed out his yard. I was on cloud nine, heading home, and this was only the beginning. When I pulled in my gate, I noticed that everybody's car was in the yard, but I hoped that they wouldn't be questioning me about my trip. I'm sure that my mom already told my dad that I went on vacation with Phoenix, so I'd be ready for the backlash. I texted Phoenix to let him know that I had made it home.

When I walked in the house, it smelled so good. The food in St. Maarten was good, but nothing compared to a home-cooked meal. I guess they heard me rolling my suitcase across the floor, so my brother and sister came out to greet me. They hugged me and filed behind me in my room. Walking in my room, I instantly got a headache, so I sat on the bed and started rubbing my throbbing temples.

"You okay, sis?" Kade asked me.

"Yeah, I just got a headache, that's all. I need some food and maybe some Bayer's aspirin."

"Okay, I'll be right back with it," Kalena said, hopping up and leaving the room.

"How was your vacation? Your black ass got a tan out of this world, lil' girl," he laughed.

"Whatever. I got you and Kalena something. Look in the small pocket of my suitcase," I told him, and fell back on the bed.

While I laid back on the bed, waiting for Kalena to come back, I watched Kade fish around in my luggage. He pulled out a black cord looking thing.

"What's this, Kam?" he asked, holding it up.

"I was getting ready to ask you what that was. I've never seen that before in my life," I replied.

Kalena came in with the medicine and a glass of water for me. I hurried and threw the pills in the back of my throat.

"Working with, … you know, I would say that this is a listening⊠"

Before Kade could finish his sentence, I jumped up and snatched it out of his hand. I rushed out the room and down the long hall to my dad's office. Even though his door was closed, I rushed into his office anyway, and threw the cord on his desk. He was on the phone, and he looked me up and down with the nastiest look.

"What is that?" I snapped.

"Um, Shaw, can I call you back in just a moment, please. A disrespectful child just walked into my office … without knocking," he said, and slammed the phone down.

He got up and came around his desk so fast, and hemmed me up against his wall. His hands found my neck, and he squeezed so hard that I felt that my brain was getting ready to ooze out of my ears. I was trying to claw at his hands, but there was nothing that I could do. He had lifted me up off the ground. I managed to kick over the small desk that was in his office, and the vase came crashing down, making the room go dark, with the only light being from the windows in his office. I was scared for my life, as I was kicking and trying to scream.

"Now, you listen to me you lil' bitch. I have let you disrespect me enough. You come home when you feel like it. You stay over at that nigga's house when you feel like it. It seems like you forgot what I was capable of doing to your ugly black ass," he growled in my face.

Just as my eyes were getting ready to close, he threw me down to the floor. I was literally trying to catch my breath. I was damn near coughing up a lung. He whisked his belt off with one yank and started tearing me up.

Whap! Whap! Whap!

"See, Kam, you make me fucking do this to you," he snapped.

I screamed out in so much pain as I felt my skin being torn open by my dad's big leather belt.

Whap! Whap! Whap!

"It's time for you to dead that relationship anyway. ... I got everything I needed from that little tape. Are you going to dead that relationship?"

"KADDEEEEEEEEE! PLEEASSEEE!" I screamed at the top of my lungs for my brother.

Whap! Whap! Whap!

"That nigga can't save you, bitch! Dead that fucking relationship. It's over!"

Kade ran into the office, shoving my dad away from me, and kneeled by my side. I could already feel my body swelling up. That beating I just got amplified the headache that I thought was going away.

Out of my eye that wasn't swollen, I could see Kalena peeking in the doorway, crying her eyes out, and my mom was standing by the door with her hands on her hip.

"Mom, can you say something to him, please? Look at Kam. She can barely move!" Kade expressed as he tried to help me up, but the pain was too unbearable.

"Well, she shouldn't have disrespected her father. I'm sure she sassed at the mouth. He don't beat her for no reason," my mom said, and I started crying even harder because I could not believe that she had said something like that.

I had never disrespected that man a day in my life, and she knew it. Kade looked from Dad to Mom, and then back to Dad.

"Come on, sis. I need to get you to the hospital," Kade said.

"You're not taking her any fucking where. Since you wanna act like her lil' boyfriend or some shit, then you can take her to the bathroom and get her cleaned up, but she ain't going to no fucking hospital, and I meant that shit. Let me find out that you went to the hospital, Kam. I'll beat you until you die, and I mean that from the bottom of my heart, and I'll get away with it," he said, and took a seat at his desk.

He sighed like beating my ass took a lot out of him. Kade wrapped my arm around his neck and picked me up on my feet. I swear it felt like my legs went numb. With the help of Kade, I hobbled toward the door.

"Like I previously said, Kambridge, you can let that relationship go anyway. Please don't force my hand, Kam. Unless you want to bury him, I suggest you end it ... tonight," he snarled at my back.

"Imagine if you had of told that bitch ass nigga you were married," Kade whispered in my ear.

Kade took me to his room and instructed Kalena to run me some bathwater, and dump alcohol, peroxide, and Epsom salt in the water. He turned the jets on in his tub. He left out while Kalena helped me get undressed, and sat me in the hot water. That shit burned to high heaven when I first sat in the water. We let the water run up to my neck. I laid a towel over my breasts and between my legs. Ten minutes later, Kade walked back in the bathroom and sat on the toilet, while Kalena sat on the edge of his tub.

I laid back and the tears started rolling down my face.

"What did I ever do to him? I've never done anything to him. I'm always respectful towards him. Always," I cried out.

"Kam. I'm going to get us out of here. I've already been looking at condos, but I haven't applied for anything yet. I don't know what type of plans you and Phoenix got, but I need to get you out of here. I can't believe that dude said those things to you like we weren't even standing there, and then Mom was standing there with her hands on her hips like what he does to you is normal. I have never heard you get out of line with him, ever." Kade expressed his feelings.

"Kade, can I come too? I'm scared of him. I don't want him to hurt me. If y'all leave me, he may kill me," Kalena said.

"Of course. I wouldn't leave you here with him. Let's let Kam soak for a little while longer," Kade replied to her.

Kade and Kalena left out the bathroom, leaving me to soak until the water turned cold. The Epsom salt made me feel a little better, and after I rubbed down in aloe vera gel, the scars didn't sting as much. I'm sure after a few pain pills, I'd be able to go to work in the morning. I dragged myself to bed without even eating. My husband kept trying to FaceTime me, but I was rejecting his phone calls. I just didn't feel like talking to anyone. I needed sleep and for this headache to go away.

∞

When I woke up the next morning, my body was not as sore as I thought it would be. I soaked in my tub for an hour, got in the shower, and rinsed off. I beat my face and threw on a pair of linen pants and a long-sleeve shirt. I was gathering my things for the day when my mom burst in the room with a tray of breakfast. I looked at my watch to make sure I was looking at the time correctly. My store opened at nine, and my mom was coming in my room at 8:30 trying to give me breakfast.

She was trying to hand me the tray, but I stared at her. I didn't know why she thought that we would be cool after how she tried to play me yesterday with Dad. Although my stomach was rumbling, I wouldn't give her the satisfaction.

"Kambridge, I made you breakfast. Can you at least pretend that you care and eat some of it?" she said.

"Nah, I'm good. Go give it to Dad. Why you ain't on your way to work anyway? It's way after eight."

"Um, I'm going to start going in later so I can cook you and your sister and brother some breakfast."

"Mom, why did you say that yesterday? *She probably sassed her dad,*" I mocked her. "You know I have never ever sassed that man and that he beats me for no reason."

"Kam, can you have a seat, please? I want to talk to you for a second," she said.

I sat in the chair at my desk, and she sat on my bed. She clasped her hands together in front of her as if she was nervous about what she was getting ready to say.

"Um, Kalena told me that you and Phoenix got married when you were in St. Maarten. Now⌧"

"Kalena would never betray me," I cut her off.

"Now, I don't know if you did that to defy your father, but if you promise to get an annulment, I won't tell your father, but if you don't, then I won't hesitate to tell him. I told you that you guys were moving too fast. Kam, he is almost thirty, and you are not even twenty-five yet. What are you going to do with that man? You guys are on two different levels and..."

"Are you done, Mom? He makes me happy, and we are going to be together for the rest of our lives, and I mean that. I don't know what your issue is with him, but we are not getting an *annulment*, so I don't care what you do with the information. Now, excuse me. I have to get to work."

"When he hurts your lil' feelings, don't come running to me," she sniped.

"Don't worry. You will be the last person that I run to about anything," I said and left out of the room.

My nerves were getting the best of me, so I called Kalena to ask her if she had told Mom about me and Phoenix getting married. Just as I suspected, Kalena said that she didn't tell Mom about it, and I believed her. Now the only thing is, I needed to figure out how she found that out. She could have found out through the listening device that my dad had in my suitcase, but that's weird as well because he never mentioned me being married to him. Something ain't right about this whole situation, and it's burning my soul to know. Sliding through the highway, jamming to Freddie Jackson, my music cut off, and my husband's name popped up on the radio.

"Good morning, baby!" I answered.

"It ain't no fucking good morning. Mane, I needed to fucking see you last night, and your ass was not picking up the phone," he snapped.

"Sorry about that, bae! As soon as I got home, I showered and got straight in the bed. I guess I was happy to be sleeping in my own bed. I didn't even wake up until this morning."

"Kambridge, don't do that shit again. Your lil' black ass should have sent me a message or something. After sleeping next to your ass for the last week, I had a hard time falling asleep. You my addiction, ma."

"Awww! I'm pulling up to my store now. I'm so ready to see you today," I said.

"I know, right? Let's start a savings account and a joint account. We can still have separate accounts though. How does that sound to you, baby?"

"That actually sounds like a plan. You know what I was thinking … We can apply for a loan at the bank for all the equipment and stuff."

Turning the key in the lock, I pushed my door opened and let out a bloodcurdling scream. I fell to my knees and continued to scream. I could hear Phoenix saying that he was on his way. I called my dad, my mom, and Kade. I laid on the floor in front of my register, pulled my knees into my chest, and started crying my eyes out. Everything was everywhere. All my glasses and mugs were smashed on the ground. There was spray paint everywhere. EVERYWHERE! I couldn't even bring myself to go to the back and see what was going on in there. I just didn't want to go in there.

"WHAT THE FUCK! BABY, WHERE YOU AT?" I heard my husband's voice as he stepped through the broken glass.

He rushed by my side to comfort me. He was rubbing my back.

"Baby, I don't bother anybody. I stay to myself. I give back to the community. I have never harmed anybody in my life. I have never even been in a fight in my life. Why would someone do this to me?" I cried while rocking myself at the same time.

"Baby, where your camera shit at? Let me go look in the back. The camera probably caught everything," he said and walked away from me.

No sooner than Phoenix walked in the back, my parents and Kade rushed through the door. Kade rushed to my side, while my mom and dad stood back staring at me. I didn't know why I called them, to be honest. I thought they would try to console me.

"Baby, whoever did this shit, fucked with … oh … Mr. and Mrs. Lewis," Phoenix acknowledged my parents, but neither of my parents spoke back to him.

"I don't know why you are down on that ground crying. Your life ain't started getting bad until you met him. You been had this store for over a year now, and no one has ever vandalized your shit, but you get with him and..." my mom started, but Phoenix cut her off.

"What are you getting at, Mrs. Lewis? To be honest, I ain't even⬚"

"Save all that shit for somebody who gives a damn. Kam, you better wake up. This nigga got hoes all over the city, and they gon' do more damage next time."

"Who my hoes, Tracey? Name at least one of my hoes, and I'll give you a thousand dollars right now," Phoenix snapped on her.

"Young man, don't talk to my wife like that. I don't know who you think you are, but I will lock your ass up for the rest of your life," my dad sniped at Phoenix.

I raised my hands up to my ears to drown out the argument that was taking place between my parents and Phoenix. I just didn't have the strength to deal with this shit right now, and what I do that for?

"KAMBRIDGE! What the fuck is that on your ankle?" Phoenix yelled.

I looked down and saw that my pants had raised a little, and there were welts on my ankles. Phoenix dropped down to one knee by me, and lifted my pants all the way up. My leg was fucked up and full of bruises. He jumped up in my dad's face.

"PUT YOUR MOTHAFUCKIN' HANDS ON KAM AGAIN! DO IT! I SWEAR TO GOD, I'LL KILL YOU!"

"You don't even have the balls to kill me. Your little threats don't scare me. You ain't shit to be honest. You are just like your⌧"

WHAP! WHAP!

Phoenix cocked back and two pieced my dad so hard, and laid him all the way out, while my mom screamed at Phoenix. Kade and I looked on in amazement because my dad was a big guy. My dad was tall and what you would describe as a thick man.

"ARE YOU OUT OF YOUR FUCKING MIND? I'M CALLING THE FUCKING POLICE! YOU GOING TO JAIL NA!" my mom screamed.

My mom pulled her phone out and stepped away from us. Kade helped me up, and I ran into my husband's arms. He hugged and kissed me. Five minutes later, my dad was getting up off the floor, looking confused until he realized that Phoenix had knocked his ass out. Five minutes after that, the cop cars came to a screeching halt outside my store.

They walked in, looking around at the store. They both had very confused looks on their faces.

"Wait a minute. Was the phone call for a vandalism or for someone hitting an officer of the court?" the first officer said.

"Him." My mom pointed at Phoenix. "He hit Judge Kason Lewis and knocked him out."

The police officers rushed over to handcuff Phoenix. They kneed him in his back, and he fell face first on the floor in front of me.

"MOM, YOU CALLED THE POLICE FOR DAD, BUT NOT FOR MY STORE BEING VANDALIZED!" I screamed at my mom.

"Judge Kason, do you want to press charges?" the police officer asked as he dug his knee deep into Phoenix's back.

"Before you answer that, Dad, I have a question for the police officer." I glared at my dad. "Mr. Police Officer, say for instance, a young lady showed up to your police station with these types of bruises on her." I raised the sleeves of my shirt up. "What would you do to that person?" I asked, and then cut my eyes to my dad.

"We would arrest them if that person wants to press charges on that person," the police officer said.

"Humph," I said rubbing my chin.

"Let him up," my dad said. The look he gave me sent chills down my spine. The hairs on my body stood up.

The police officer let Phoenix up and uncuffed him. My dad and my mom were looking like they wanted to explode.

"Now that you are here, my store was vandalized when I was on vacation, and I need to file a report," I said to the police officer.

He pulled out his notepad, and we started walking around the store, surveying the damage. Phoenix and Kade were walking along with us. My mom and dad had snuck out of the store. I'm sure that he was dying from embarrassment. I took a deep breath before I walked in the back of my store, and when I saw all the damage, I instantly got weak in my knees. My brother had to catch me. My machines were in pieces. My logo computer was smashed. I didn't even want to think of the price for all this shit.

"Ms. Lewis, I think we got everything that we need for right now. We will be in touch," the police officer said and walked away, leaving me, Phoenix, and my brother in the backroom.

My feelings were so hurt because I ain't never bothered nobody for them to do this to me. This shit seemed personal to me. I ain't know if I wanted to hire someone to clean this place up, or if I wanted to do it myself. Phoenix wrapped his arms around me and reassured me that everything was going to be okay.

Malice

Kam's shop was so fucked up, and there was only one person in mind that could have done this to my wife: Cat. On top of that shit, her daddy had put his hands on her again. Man, I lost it when I saw her scars. I promised her that I would always protect her from anybody, including her dad. That nigga had to have thought I was some scrub or something, and was going to let him talk to me any type of way. I didn't know what the fuck I was thinking, swinging on a judge … Hell, I wasn't thinking. That nigga hurt my baby, and now I had to hurt his ass. As soon as I two-pieced that nigga, his body flattened out like a stiff board, which let me know that I had knocked his ass silly. I bet he would think twice before he put his hands on Kam again, or stepped to me, for that matter.

Hours later, Kam and I were halfway done with sweeping up all the glass.

"Baby, we have to take a break so we can go to the bank," she said as she wiped the sweat from her brow.

"Kam, baby, that can wait. We have to get your shop back up and running before we worry about the building. We have to replace all the shit that was broken. There is no way that I can take money from you, knowing that we about to be out of… Give me a ballpark figure, bae. How much you think all this is going to cost?"

"Ummm, if I had to give you a ballpark figure …" she looked around. "… I would say about twenty-five thousand dollars. Those machines were very expensive. Don't worry about that, I can get a loan from the bank. I don't want to file this on the insurance because the premium will go up, and I don't have time for it. I will put it in both of our names so we can start building some type of credit as a union."

She started sweeping the glass to the middle of the store. I stared at my wife in disbelief because I couldn't believe that God would bless me with someone like her. My life had been so crazy by far, and God still showed up and showed out for me. Her store had been destroyed, but she was still trying to help me get my shit up and running.

"Hey, bae?" she called out to me.

"What's up, mama?"

"Why do bad things happen to good people? I have never done anything to anybody, ever. I love my family, but my dad can't keep his hands off me. I love my store, and I charge the cheapest I can for these shirts and things, and someone still vandalized my store. I feed the homeless whenever I see them. I donate my old clothes and shoes to shelters. I've never harmed anyone, so why would someone do this to me?" she said, and the tears started rolling down her eyes.

It sounded like she was defeated. My baby sounded like she was tired, and I felt my body starting to heat up because there was nothing I could do to make her feel better. Before I could say anything, she continued to vent. I leaned on the broom and listened intensely as my wife spoke. The look in her eyes as she stared into mine, fucked with my heart bad.

"All I ever wanted was for my dad to love me. To say that he was proud of me. To say that he loved me. If it wasn't for Kade, I would swear that physical abuse means love. I've never disrespected him. Ever. I just don't understand why he does that to me. I had perfect attendance in school ... never skipped a day. Even when it hurt for me to sit down, hurt for me to write, hurt for me to even open my eyes sometimes, I was there in school. Graduated valedictorian, and I couldn't even celebrate with the few friends I had because my body was throbbing. Graduated at the TOP of my college class. Do you know how many people attend a graduation? A college graduation? In my graduating class, there were 600 students. Out of 600 students, I graduated top twenty. Imagine how hard that was, and that very night, I got the brakes beat off me for not coming in at twelve."

"But, ma, why didn't..."

"Didn't I call CPS?" she finished my question, and I nodded my head. "Call CPS for what? I don't think you know how powerful my dad really is. That wouldn't have done a thing to him."

"You're moving in with me. I bet his ass won't come get you from my house. If he steps foot on my property, I'll kill that mothafucka, baby. You're moving in with me, and I mean that, a'ight? Don't go back to that house. Let's finish sweeping this glass up, go to the bank, and then go lay down. I can run you a hot bath and give you a good massage, and you can get a good night's rest. Is that okay, mama?"

She smiled a little bit, and then nodded her head.

"To answer your question though, bad things happen to good people because that's how the world works, baby. Innocent people die and go to jail all the time because that is how the world works. How can we fully enjoy joy, if we have never experienced pain? How can we truly experience happiness, if we have never experienced sadness? How can we truly enjoy love if we have never experienced a few bad apples? Kambridge, you can either let the bad shit destroy you or strengthen you. The Kambridge *I* know … *my* beautiful wife … is not going to let this shit get to her. WE are going to have this shit up and running in no time. I can promise you that."

She ran into my arms, and I gave her the biggest hug that I knew she needed. After we finished sweeping up the glass, we headed to the bank. She didn't want me to completely wipe out my savings, so I was going to use 150 thousand dollars of my money, and she was going to give me fifty thousand of her money. It truly bothered me getting fifty thousand from my wife, but she showed me her bank statement, and her store was doing good. Better than I thought, to be honest. She was going to get a loan to repair her store, and after the building was purchased, we were going to slowly work on fixing the building up. The first start was going to be the contractor coming out to see how he could fix it up, and we were going to go from there.

As much as it pained me, I was going to have to ask Mayhem for some money because I hadn't been fucking with nobody since I realized that I had been fucking Kam's mama. That shit low key traumatized the fuck out of me. Plus, Kam was my wife now, and that tight ass pussy would be the only pussy that I stuck my dick in for the rest of my life.

I cut my eyes at her as we were riding to the bank. She was bobbing her head to the music, looking cute as fuck. Twenty minutes later, we pulled into the bank, and surprisingly, it was not packed. We walked in the bank, got checked in, and immediately got pissed off when I realized that Susan, one of my old clients, had called us into her office. I said a small prayer that she'd be cool, as she escorted us into her office. I walked in after Kam, so she glared at me when I walked by her. She was one of the ones that I had to cancel the standing appointments with after I gave Kam my last name.

"So, what can I help you with today?" she asked no one in particular, but kept her eyes on me.

I looked at my wife, but she was looking down at her phone, sending the last text message, before putting her phone in her purse.

"We are going to start a joint account and a savings account, and I want to apply for a loan."

"I didn't know friends did that type of thing," she laughed. "Or are you guys classmates?" She smiled, picking up her coffee mug.

"No, we're married," Kam spoke.

She spit out the coffee and started choking on what was left of it. I cut my eyes at Kam, and she was raising an eyebrow at her. I gave her the eye like 'bitch, you better not say nothing crazy.'

"Oh, wow! Congratulations. I just didn't have an inkling of you two being married. You two look so young, and plus, you are not wearing your rings. How long have you guys been married?"

"Just a week. We got married in St. Maarten." Kam smiled and pulled out a picture of us at the courthouse in our white ensembles. I could tell that she was really excited to show Susan the picture of us.

"Oh, okay. Wow! Well, let me get you guys started on your accounts. How much are you going to start with in your joint account and your savings account?" Susan asked.

"Well, we are going to start with five thousand in our joint account, and ten in our savings account. You can move twenty-five hundred from our separate accounts into the joint account, and five from each account into the savings," Kam spoke.

My wife was so fucking smart. I mean, I knew talking about money and accounts was simple, but the way she was so confident when she talked turns me on so fucking much. I was admiring her so much that I hadn't realized that Susan was telling me where I had to sign.

"Now, I want to fill out an application for a loan for twenty-five thousand dollars," Kam said.

"What do you need it for?"

"Shop repairs. My shop was vandalized, and I have to repair it. Would it be okay if I put my husband on this loan with me? It will be great credit building for us both."

"What is it that your husband does?" Susan leaned back in her chair and stared at me.

"Well, he cuts hair."

"Interesting. How is he going to help you pay the loan back if he only *cuts hair*?"

I felt my body getting hot because I wasn't sure if she was about to blow my spot up or not.

"Well..." Kam started, but Susan cut her off.

"Are you sure that's all he does? I mean, I'm looking here at over two hundred thousand dollars in his account. There is no way one person made that much money just from *cutting hair*," she said.

"Mrs. Susan, I'm not sure what you are implying, but my husband came from a very good and well-off family. He has never done any of the things that you are implying. If you can give me an application for the loan, and I'll speak to someone else regarding your behavior towards my husband. I'm not sure if you are having a bad day or not, but⌧"

Kam stopped talking once I put my hand on her thigh.

"Mrs. Susan, is there anything else that you need from us?" I asked her.

She told us that we had to fill out the application online and that we would have an answer in a week or so. We got up and left the office. Today had been a day, and I was in the same boat as Kam … just needing to get in the bed, and try again tomorrow.

"Baby, do you want to go to the realtor's office, or do you want to wait another day?" I asked her.

"Yeah, let's just get everything out the way today. I'm so tired, and I just want to go home, get in the tub, and then go to sleep," she replied.

We rode in silence to Bernie's office. She linked her hand in mine and kept kissing it. I didn't know why she did that, but I truly appreciated when she did. Pulling into the office, I got out and opened the door for her. When we walked in the office, Bernie looked at me like he had a seen a ghost. I could not read his expression, but I could tell that it wasn't good. I hoped that the owner of the building hadn't raised the price on it. He ushered me and Kam into his office, and he took a seat behind his desk.

"I came to tell you that it's a go on the building. I'm going to purchase it," I said.

"I'm sorry, son, but I sold the building. The person offered me three hundred racks, and I couldn't turn that down. I'm truly sorry," he said.

"You've been working with me for the last few months on that, and you sold the building?" I asked through gritted teeth. "Who did you sell the building to?"

"I can't release that type of information," he said.

"Kam, can you go wait in the car for me, please? Please don't ask any questions. Just go. I'll be right behind you."

Kam eased out the door, and since his office had a big window, I could see the car from the window. I waited until she was in the car, before I reached over the desk and snatched him up by the collar, and pulled his fat ass across the desk.

"Who did you sell the building to? This is going to be my last time asking," I growled.

"Um … um … Catherine Jenson. She bought it last week," he stuttered. "Um, um, um, she is a white⊠"

"Thank you very much," I said.

I threw him down on the floor, and rushed out the building to the car. I sat in the driver's seat and stared at the building. I was so pissed that I didn't even have any words.

"Phoenix, it is going to be alright. We will find another building," she whispered.

"Nah, I wanted that building, and I'm going to get it. But let me get you home and to bed. You have had a long afternoon, and I know you just want to get to bed so we can start over tomorrow."

The whole ride to my house, I was fuming, but I had to hide it from my wife. Today turned out to be just as bad of a day for me as it was for my wife. First, Tracey's stupid ass trying to turn Kam against me, Susan's ass low-key trying to blow up my spot, and lastly, Cat buying the building that I had been working on trying to purchase for the longest. Today had been a day, and it was only going to get worse because after I put my wife to bed, I was going to pay Cat Jenson a visit.

Cat

Taking several sips of wine, I looked at Kam's updated page on social media, and saw that she had Malice as her Facebook header. The sunset was pretty, and I clicked on the picture. The location says the picture was taken in St. Maarten, so that meant that Malice and his bitch were vacationing. Silly me for even feeling one ounce of bad after purchasing that building. That's probably why his ass hadn't been over to my place yet because he didn't know that I bought the building.

One other thing that was weird was that all of Malice's clients that I knew personally, were calling me, telling me that he had cancelled their appointments with no explanation, and I texted him to ask him about it, but he didn't respond. So, I looked in his phone at his calendar, and sure enough, all his appointments were cancelled. He hadn't been responding to none of my texts lately, and I knew it was because of that bitch. What the fuck could she do in four or five months that I hadn't done in twelve fucking years? Malice had me messed up if he thought that I was going to really let that girl just take him away from me.

After my third glass of wine, I got a phone call from Susan. She had been a client of Malice's for about three years. He would fuck her on Mondays and Fridays, for four thousand dollars. That bitch loved for Malice to fuck her in her ass. She got off on that shit. Malice and I tried that a few times because eventually, he would have to cut all those bitches off so we could be together, and I wanted to be able to fully please him.

"Hello," I finally picked up the phone.

I prayed that she wasn't calling me because of the cancellations because that didn't have shit to do with me, and I didn't feel like explaining it again as I had to the last five bitches that called me.

"Um, hey, it's Susan," she said like I didn't have caller ID.

"Hey, girl! What's going on?" I asked in the fakest voice that I could muster.

"Interesting thing happened today. Malice came by with a young girl. Black girl. She said that they were married. They were opening up savings accounts and joint accounts. They got married in St. Maarten ..." She paused momentarily. "... And it's very much real," she whispered.

The large lump in my throat grew before I could even swallow the spit that was in my mouth. I could barely breathe. The water built up in my eyes as she continued to rant on. I didn't quite understand anything after the word married. I didn't think my mind could truly process anything after that word. I was holding the phone in my hand, but my soul had left my body. Without blinking, the water slid down my face. At some point, Susan had hung up the phone. Jumping at the sound of the phone against my ear, I looked at it, and it was Connor. I wanted to answer. I needed to answer, but I was frozen in place. He probably was calling me to tell me about the bar exam.

Everything was in slow motion after that phone call. I slowly pulled the covers back on my bed, and got under them. I set the phone on the nightstand, and just laid there. I was so hurt. I closed my eyes, and eventually fell asleep.

The minute I felt the cold steel pressed against my forehead, my eyes popped open. I was staring into Malice's eyes. His eyes were dark and cold. His eyes were very unreadable, and for the first time in twelve years, I feared him. Even when he choked me out and threw me to the ground, my pussy got wet, but now, he had a gun pointed to my forehead with his finger on the trigger.

"Catherine," he called my name. His voice was low and just above a whisper. "Give me one good reason why I shouldn't cover your expensive sheets with brain matter!" he said, and cocked the gun.

"Phoenix ... what ... what ..." I started.

"Don't call me that! You lost all those privileges when you started fucking with me. You bought the fucking building that I had been looking at. Cat, I trusted you. Trusted you with everything, but this is the way you ... Give me a fucking reason why I shouldn't blast your ass. You buy the building, and then you fuck up my wife's store. The fuck is wrong with you."

My eyes darted from side to side because I was confused. I had only been inside of her store one time.

"Malice, I never fucked up your little ... wait a minute ... did you just call her your wife?" I gasped.

I knew Susan told me that he was married, but to hear him comfortably call her his wife, made my skin crawl. My insides turned, my mouth got wet, and I could feel myself getting ready to throw up. The little throw up that came up into my throat, I swallowed it because I didn't want to make any sudden movements with this gun to my head.

"Yeah, my wife. I married her. I'm in love with her, but that's not what I'm here for. Why the fuck is you playing with me?" he snapped.

"Look." I held my hands up. "I didn't fuck up her store. That's not my style. You know the only reason I'm ever getting sweaty is when I'm riding your cock!" I said, and inched my hands to his dick to start stroking it through his pants he was wearing.

Reluctantly, he let me. I could see his jaw line moving, meaning he was getting turned on. He held his head back and let out a little moan. I knew I had him, or so I thought. He moved back just when I was getting ready to inch his dick out of his pants.

"Why the fuck did you fuck with Kam's store? I know you did it," he repeated himself.

"Malice, I promise you that I didn't mess with *that girl's* store. You are acting like I'm the only woman that you are having..."

"You are the only woman that would want to ruin my fucking life. You already bought the building that I had my eye on for a while. It ain't no telling what you're capable of," he growled.

You're right about that, I thought.

I let out a sigh of relief when he eased the gun away from my head and back to his side.

"Cat, I tried to continue to be friends with you. I tried to let you down easy, but you keep fucking with me. Now, everything is over. All contact is..."

"Malice!!" I screeched, raising up, and attaching myself to his waist.

He backed away, but I kept my arms around his waist, and he dragged me out of the bed.

"What do I have to do?" I asked. "I'll sell you the building for half the price, if I can keep our friendship. Just our friendship. We have come too far to end this way, and you know that."

"Nah, I'm good. Just stay away from me. Stay away from my wife and anything that involves me. I mean that from the last lil' spot in my heart that I have for you. You got one last chance, Cat. Next time, I'll pull the trigger," he said, and left out the door.

I had cried my last tear for Phoenix Bailey, and he was truly going to wish that he hadn't fucked with me.

Trent Wilson (Big Will)

I laid on my bed and stared at the ceiling with my hands clasped behind my head. Twenty-two years. Twenty-fucking-two years is how long I have been behind these bars. True enough, the drugs are what got me behind the bars, but the REAL reason I was behind bars is because I fell in love with a hoe! It's crazy because something in my fucking stomach told me not to approach that hoe, but I did anyway, especially since she had her son with her. After twenty plus years, I had never approached nor dated a woman with kids, but I made an exception for her.

When I first saw her, I didn't know who she was, but later that week when she was riding my dick, she told me that her husband was all over the TV, so we had to be discreet. I should have left her DUMB ASS alone THEN! That was the sign that God gave me. Only one of many that my dumb ass ignored. I kept fucking with her. I heard that she had been fucking other niggas in the hood, but I ignored it. The pussy was so fucking good that my dumb ass got sprung, unintentionally. I got her pregnant, and I didn't know why I thought that we were going to be together, but I was fucking wrong. On some bitch nigga shit, I told her that I would blow her spot up if she got rid of the baby.

I showed up at the hospital when she was born, and that's when my life took a turn for the worse. That nigga locked me up, and I've been here ever since. Tracey sent me one picture of her, and that's when she cut off all communication with me. The only pictures I have of her now, is the pictures of her and her family that's been in the local magazines. Kambridge's business was also featured in this magazine for best new businesses in Chicago. She was so beautiful, and I swear that she only has a few of my features. Korupt sent me a few pictures of her at both graduations.

"Big Will, the warden needs to see you," the CO said at the door.

I was confused because I ain't bothered nobody. Sure, I still made my money while I was locked up, but I ain't never bothered nobody in here. For the most part, people feared me, and the minute I stepped foot in this bitch, everybody, including guards, was trying to make me comfortable.

"For what?" I asked.

"Shit, I don't know, fam! He just said that he needed to see you," he replied.

I got up, slipped on my shoes, and followed him down the hall. On the way, I saw a few familiar faces, but one made me stop in my tracks.

"Frank, what the hell are you doing in here?" I asked.

I nodded my head and told him to follow me into the corner. The C.O. stood there while I talked to Frank.

"Mane, I just got transferred in here when a bed became available. Kason put me in here. That nigga getting crazier and crazier. We have to expose that nigga sooner or later, and then drop his ass," he whispered. "Korupt said that once he gets his shit back, he's going to off the whole family in a house fire or some shit like that, Mayhem told me," Frank said.

"The whole family?" I asked for clarification because I knew Korupt wasn't going to kill my daughter.

"Yeah … the whole family. We not going to be in here much longer," he spoke.

I was beyond pissed, and couldn't wait to get back to my bed to call that nigga because he ain't run that shit by me, and if he touched one hair on my daughter, I would break out this bitch and kill him— friend or not.

"Thanks for the update, fam! Stay up. Ain't nobody gon' bother you in here. Know that!" I said, and dapped him up.

The C.O. continued to lead me to the warden's office. Once I got in there, I continued to stand even after he offered me a seat.

"Um, I don't know how to say this. Trent, I had become the warden here when you had just walked through the doors. So, we've roughly been here the same time. To me, you have been a stellar inmate, and I just⊠"

"Spit it out, man. You making me nervous," I chuckled.

"Well, I just got word from the governor that you are going to be transferred down to Arkansas when the first bed becomes available. They didn't give me a reason after I asked several times. I swear I spoke on your behalf, … practically begged for you to stay in your place here, but the governor said that his hands were tied in this situation."

I felt like the wind had been knocked out of me, and I had to take a seat. I wasn't afraid to go to a new prison, but damn, I'd been here twenty-two years. Out of all the people they could have moved, … they moved me, which leads me to believe that I was targeted. There was only one person who would want me moved, and that was Kason. The question is why now?

"Thank you for talking on my behalf. I'm sure that you did everything you could to keep me here," I said to him, and shook his hand.

That nigga's palm was sweaty as hell, which was a sign of nervousness.

"Relax, I believe you, and I won't have you touched. When do you think the bed will open down there? Do I have time to let my family know?"

"Yeah, I don't think a bed will open up down there for another six months, so everything is okay right now. I still have six months to plead your case."

I nodded my head and walked out of the office. The C.O. was still waiting there for me, and he told me that I had a visitor as well. I didn't have an idea who it could be because Korupt said that he wasn't going to be able to make it today, so he was going to come later this week. When I walked out into the visitor's room, it was my godson, Malice. He stood, and I gave him a hug because I hadn't seen him in months, but we talked frequently.

"Why you ain't tell me you were coming? I would have dressed up," I joked with him.

He laughed. In just a few months, he had changed. I scanned over his appearance. He still looked the same, but I could tell that he was stressed out about something. I took a mental note to talk to him about what was going on.

"Uncle, I came here so you could meet my wife. I know I should have let you meet her before I married her, but I was itching for her to have my last name. Like, I feel myself becoming obsessed with her. She is the air that I breathe. My life has changed so drastically since I got with her. I even changed my whole life around for her. I'll have to talk to you about that later."

"Well, hell, where is she? She got you over here talking like a simp ass nigga," I asked.

"She went to the bathroom, and she should be out in a minute." He grinned like he was happy I was about to meet her. "Oh, there she is."

When I looked up, my heart stopped. My breath was caught in my throat as I watched her command the attention of the other prisoners and their family. I could feel my temper rise because I knew that my baby was going to be the reason a lot of these niggas got their nuts off tonight. Her hair was big and thick, like mine. She even had two big braids in the center of her hair, and the rest was fluffed out. I could only imagine how traumatized she must have been because of the way I'm sure they checked her hair. I felt as if the walls were closing in on me the closer she got to us. I stood up when she made it to the table, and she pulled me in for a hug.

"I'm sorry, sir. I'm a hugger." She laughed and took a seat next to Malice. "You smell really good by the way," she leaned in and whispered. "I didn't know people in prison could have cologne. Like, I wouldn't want to smell good for other men. I've seen prison movies before." Malice nudged her, and she twisted up her lips before whispering sorry to me.

"My bad, Uncle. ... My wife watches too much TV. She's never even had BBQ before, just to put things into context," Malice joked. "But anyways, Trent, this is my wife, Kambridge Bailey, and Kam, this is my godfather, but I call him uncle, Trent Wilson."

"I love your hair, by the way. You braid it yourself? It's really long. I have so many questions. I don't know if you want to answer them or not," she blurted out.

"Kambridge, baby, I'll answer any question that you would like for me to answer," I replied to her, and her eyes lit up.

"Save the questions for later, baby girl. Matter of fact, let me talk to him alone for a second. Give me about ten minutes and come back, okay?" he said, kissing her on her lips.

We both watched her walk away. She was shaped just like her mom: long legs and petite.

"Uncle, I need your help. I need some solid advice. I don't have time to tell you the whole story, but long story short, I am ... was a male escort. Don't look like that, I needed money. I'd been doing this since I was sixteen, and I had over two hundred thousand dollars saved up. This old white woman, Cat, is who put me on, but she ain't taking me being with Kam lightly. She's trying to ruin my life. She bought the building that Kam and I were looking to purchase. She showed up to her store and got a shirt made with my initials on it, but Kam's so oblivious, that she ain't think nothing of it, but that's only one third of the problem. She knows that Kam doesn't know, and I believe she's been fucking with us ever since. Okay, listen, this is going to sound mmmaaddd crazy, but I fucked Kam's mom too, and Cat knows about it. I'm terrified that Cat is going to expose me, and Kam is going to divorce me," he said. It seemed like he said it in one big breath.

"What the fuck?" I shouted, but then quieted down when the C.O.'s shot me a look.

"Listen, I didn't know at first until Kam invited me over for dinner, man. I haven't talked to her mom since. After we got married, I quit being a male escort, and as much as it pains me, I'mma have to ask Mayhem for some money. Her mom calls and texts me from different numbers, talking about she just wants to continue to fuck me without me telling Kam. She said that she will pay me double, which would be six thousand dollars, to keep knocking her off."

"Son..."

"I know. Terrible, terrible, terrible dilemma I'm in, but I'm in love with Kam. Like, Unc, I can't lose her over this bullshit. She has been my rock. She's been putting me up on business game, and she even wants to open up a business together with me. Unc, I'm going to hurt her, and it's going to kill me to do so. Is there a way to get out of telling her? Maybe I can just move her out the city, and we can start over. Her dad already doesn't like me, and he's made that clear. I had to knock his ass out a few days ago. Man, Cat vandalized her store, and then her mom and dad came in talking about she needs to leave me alone, and then he tried to talk shit to me. I knocked his ass out. I moved her in with me though because he can't keep his hands off her."

I felt my blood pressure rising at the vision I got of Kason putting his hands on my daughter. At this point, I wanted to tell Malice everything, but I just couldn't. Not right now. He needed me, and not to drop a bombshell like this on him.

"You know the crazy thing about all of that, Unc. That girl used to think that love was getting knocked around. She still loves that fool, even though she talks about him not loving her. I don't know what to do," he ranted.

Taking a deep breath, I replied, "You have to tell her, and let the chips fall where they may. Life happens, and if it's meant for you guys to be together, you will be together, and nothing will stop that. I kinda knew that's what you were doing to get money; your dad mentioned it a couple of times, but I ain't think anything of it. You had to do what you had to do, and Kam will understand that part. Will she understand that you slept with her mom? Probably not, and it will take her a while to get over it."

"The bad part of all of this is that I lied in the beginning. I told her that I didn't know Cat, and to find out that I've been fucking her since I was a teenager, is going to hurt as well. I tried to leave her alone after I found out that Tracey was her mom, but my heart wouldn't let me do that. It kept drawing me to her. Kam's heart is like a magnet. Maybe I shouldn't have married her. After all, I was just supposed to use her at first. I'm sure my dad already told you about the situation."

"Maybe you shouldn't have. Everything about this relationship is built on lies. Sure, you love her, and I don't doubt that. The way you look at her shows that you love her, but you should have waited until you told her how you got money," I said to him. "Follow me out here.

It's been more than ten minutes, and she hasn't shown back up."

We got up and walked outside. Kam was sitting Indian style on the ground with kids, drawing on the concrete with chalk. They were laughing and giggling as if they'd known Kam all their lives. I nodded my head at Ray. He only got two years, and should be getting out soon. His grandma brought his kids to visit him faithfully. Just like me, he was in here over a woman and their bullshit.

"You're so pretty, Ms. Kam. Can you be my daddy's girlfriend when he gets out?" his daughter asked.

"JENN!" Ray yelled at her, but Jenn shrugged her shoulders, not paying attention to her dad.

Kam chuckled. "I'm sorry, Jenn, but I have a husband. I may have the perfect girl for him when he gets out, though."

"I bet your husband is not as cute as my dad."

"Miss Jenn, are you trying to give my wife away?" Malice asked and squatted behind Kam.

She turned around and looked at Malice as if she had seen a ghost. She whispered in Kam's ear, making her laugh, and then went and sat next to her dad. I walked them back in, and we took a seat at the table.

"Jenn said that she didn't want to make her dad jealous, but you are much cuter than her dad. I love little kids, man," Kam laughed.

"So, Mrs. Bailey, tell me about yourself. I need to know if you can take care of my nephew over here," I said to her.

"Well, I would like to think that I have his best interest at heart. To many people, we may not have the ideal relationship, because heck, we only met like four or five months ago, and now we are married. But, Mr. Wilson, it feels so right. He takes care of me mentally and physically. Although, when we first met, he was such an asshole to me, and I low key hated him. He's showing me a different world, just as I am showing him a different world. Once we get our own place, he won't have to do anything but bring home the bacon, and I'll do the rest. Well, I'mma still be bringing home the bacon too, but you get what I'm saying," she said, and then turned to him, but kept speaking to me. "I'm going to make life much easier for him. He won't have to cook or clean, unless he wants to. I'm truly committed and submissive to him," she said.

"Kammm, can I have a hug? I have to go," Jenn said.

Kam got up, picked her up, and hugged her tight.

"How am I supposed to tell her some shit like that after what she just said?" Malice whispered to me.

I shrugged because even I didn't have an answer to that question. She sat back down, and we continued to talk for two more hours. If I ain't get anything else from this visit, I got that my baby is kind of like me. She's talkative, and she always has a lot to say. She's very smart. So, Tracey and Kason did something right. She was so comfortable with me to even discuss the abuse that she suffered at home and how happy she is that she moved with Malice. I didn't even want this visit to end. She asked several crazy questions about the prisons she has saw on TV, and she looked shocked when I told her that prison on TV is definitely different than prison in real life.

"It was really nice to meet you, Mr. Wilson," she said as the C.O. yelled that we had ten minutes. "Maybe Malice can bring me back to visit you. Do you have family here besides Phoenix's dad?"

"Yeah, I do, but we can save that for later," I said. "Well, I have about six months left here before I get moved to Arkansas. So, make sure you come back soon," I said.

"What!" Malice said and sat back down. "Does Dad know?"

"Nah, they just told me this morning. I haven't had time to talk to him," I replied.

"My dad is a judge. Maybe I can ask him to move someone else instead of you. I like talking to you. You are a good listener," Kam spoke.

I wanted to tell her that Kason is the reason why I'm here, but I didn't.

"NO! Baby, don't do that, okay? Promise me that you won't mention your visit here," I said to her.

"Mr. Wilson, I don't want you to have to move. You've only been here for as long as I have been alive. I'm sure they are moving you for no reason, so I won't promise you that I won't say anything," she replied.

"Trust me, Unc! When her mind is set on something, it's hard to change it," Malice said.

We walked over to the picture area, and took several pictures before I watched them walk towards the exit. She turned around and gave me a wave and a smile that I would never forget. She made my eyes well up with tears, and that was something that hadn't happened to me in years. For some odd reason, just seeing her today let me know that there are better days ahead.

Malice

My wife and I were sitting in this tux shop watching me get my suit tailored for the Playa's Ball this weekend. I had been trying to get my wife to go, but she said that I ain't tell her in enough time to get her a fye ass dress. I told her that she would look beautiful in any dress, but not my Kambridge. She said nah. She has to be the best dressed in the place. I looked in the mirror, and I saw her typing away and smiling in her phone.

"Who got you smiling in your phone like that, woman?" I asked her.

"Well, Mr. Wilson sent me an email, so I'm emailing him back, and telling him about Mayhem fixing up my shop. Mr. Wilson is such a funny guy, and he's had an interesting life with your dad. When can we go see him again?"

Trent and Kam got along just fine at the visit. They talked as if she knew him all her life.

"Probably next weekend because you know school starts back Monday. Damn, in just a few months, I will have a Bachelor's degree. I'm so happy. I been working my ass off for this moment," I said.

"Baby, I am so very proud of you. God works on His time … not yours," she said, looking up at me. "You looking good in that tux. I might make you late the night of the ball. Hell, I might not let you go because you are looking too damn good," she said.

"Whatever. My mom told me to ask you what you wanted to eat tonight. You know we are going to dinner over there," I told her.

We were supposed to had been gone over there for dinner, but Kam had been scared out of her mind. For whatever reason, she thought that my mom was not going to like her, especially with her being the first woman I took home, and not only was she the first woman for me to take home, she was my wife. If I know my mom, she was going to be boiling on the inside, but she wouldn't show it.

"I'm not sure. Anything that she cooks will be fine with me," she said.

"Okay, ma! I'm done here. You need to stop somewhere before we head home?"

She shook her head. It felt good to be saying home. Although my brother lived there, he didn't get mad about it. Well, she only been there for a week, but she cooked and cleaned with no complaints. Like, if I made it home before her, she would walk in and kiss me passionately. If she made it home before me, I would walk in to a hot meal on the stove, and the shower already going. When I get out the shower, Kam would massage my feet. I ain't never had my feet massaged. Like, the first time she did that shit, my dick got hard as fuck. I have NEVER had my feet massaged, not because they are ugly or anything, but I just haven't. Cat had not even massaged my feet, and she claimed to love a nigga from the depths of her soul.

Speaking of Cat, she hadn't hit me up since I left her house that night, which was a good and a bad thing. A good thing because I didn't have to lie about who kept calling me anymore, and bad because I knew she wasn't done fucking with me. Tracey still hit me up at least twice a day now. Ever since my visit with Trent, I had been thinking real hard about telling her what happened. Every time I got the courage, I'd chicken out. I hadn't prayed this much in a long time. I prayed when I woke up, and when I went to sleep. I prayed that she didn't leave me after I told her.

"Baby, you okay? You are staring at me all weird like," she said as I opened the car door for her.

"Yeah, I'm good. I just love looking at your beautiful ass," I said to her.

We drove home in silence, and when we pulled up to our home, there were police cars surrounding my house. I couldn't even pull in my driveway. I had to park like five cars down. I told Kam to stay in the car, but she said no, and I didn't feel like arguing with her at this point. My first thought was that Mayhem had gotten caught up in some damn shit. We would be good because Mayhem don't bring none of that shit to the house, and they wouldn't even find a blunt.

"What's happening, baby?" Kam asked me, and held on to my arm.

"There they are! There they are!" the police yelled and started rushing us.

I moved Kam behind me, so if them bastards were about to shoot, they would shoot me first.

"GET YOUR HANDS ABOVE YOUR HEAD! GET YOUR HANDS ABOVE YOUR HEAD!" the police shouted at me, and my hands instantly went above my head.

One of the officers yanked me away from Kam and hit me with the baton, making me hit my knees. Kam was instantly trying to get by my side, but the police was holding her back, and she started screaming crying as she kept fighting with the officer to break away.

"What is going on? Why the fuck you pigs hemming me up like this? I ain't did shit," I snapped.

Nobody was answering the questions, so before I could answer, three black trucks pulled up leaving skid marks in the road from breaking real hard. Several men got out, and one of them opened the back door. Guess who stepped out? … Kason. He eased his way over to me, and ordered one of his henchmen to put the gun to my head.

"You a fucking pussy! You a fucking pussy! All of this because I knocked your ass out," I spat. "Did y'all weak ass boss tell y'all that?" I looked around at the men in black.

"Mr. Bailey, you are under arrest for kidnapping my daughter⬛"

"DADDD!" Kam screamed.

"Nigga, what the fuck! I ain't kidnap her. She came because she wanted to come. She needed to come to get away from your bitch ass," I shouted, and then spit at his foot. He moved it back just in time for it to not hit his shoes.

"Kam, baby girl, do you know how many years this young man can get for kidnapping someone, and holding them against their will? All of this can go away if you end this relationship, now!" her dad said to her. "Or … If you feel jail is not enough, or you can't leave his ass alone, then his brain matter will be spread across this concrete. Your choice, Kambridge."

Kam looked between her father and me. Her eyes were already swollen from crying so much.

"Dad, why are you doing this to me … to us? He makes me happy. I can't do this. He is the love of my life. He is my⊠" She started to call me her husband.

"I don't give a fuck how you feel about him. He is not good enough for you. Jail, dead, or end this relationship, NOW! Choose. You got three seconds," her dad commanded.

"ONE!" he counted.

Kam fell to her knees and started wheezing. When she got frustrated like this, she couldn't think.

"TWO!" he bellowed.

Click! The gun clicking made Kam scream even louder.

"Dad, please!" Kam whispered. "I love him!"

"TH..."

"Kam, it's over!" I cut him off.

I had to do something. I couldn't stand to see my baby like that.

"What, baby, no! No! It's not over." Kam ran and grabbed me around my neck.

I was trying my hardest not to break out in tears. I couldn't let this coward ass nigga know that Kam was truly my weakness. I couldn't let him see that he was getting to me. I placed both of my hands on her face and brought her in for a kiss.

"Yes, baby, it is. Your dad doesn't want me around you, and I must respect that. Just know that I love you, and I will always love you. I'm so sorry that we didn't work out, okay. I'm so sorry," I said, wrapping my arms around her.

"See how easy that was, Mr. Bailey?" Kason smirked. "Now, Kambridge, get your dumb ass up and get in the truck. You got me down here embarrassing myself because you out here wanting to be a hoe," he growled at Kam.

He yanked Kam by the collar of her shirt, and started dragging her. It was like my jaw muscles clenched on their own.

I love you, I mouthed to her before he picked her up and threw her in the truck.

Once the truck was out of sight, the police beat my ass until I passed out.

∞

Mayhem and I watched my dad pace the floor with both guns in his hands, as my mom and our on-call doctor, nursed my wounds. When I woke up, Mayhem told me that he found me outside our house, beaten badly. The more my mom and the doctor nursed my wounds, the more they burned. My whole body hurt. It hurt so bad to the point where I couldn't really pinpoint where I hurt the most.

"Son, didn't I tell you to leave that girl alone. She ain't shit but trouble," my dad said.

"Dad, you did not tell me to leave her alone. You only told me to leave her alone after you realized I fell in love with her," I talked as loud as I could.

"Well, I'm telling you now. You need to leave her alone. Her dad is not going to let you be with her in peace. You saw the shit he pulled today? He would have never pulled that shit back in the day. He a pussy, and I can't wait to get my fucking hands on him. He fucking playing with me."

"Did you talk to Uncle Trent? They are moving him to Arkansas. You know we went to visit him. I took Kam to meet him, and they instantly clicked."

"I haven't talked to him in a few days, but ... wait a minute, you did what?" he asked me again as if he didn't hear me the first time.

"Kam and I went to visit him."

"No, no, no, no, no," my dad said, and shook his head at the same time.

"What's going on, Korupt?" I asked him.

"You need to leave her alone, son. Did Big Will tell you anything?"

"No, what was he supposed to tell me?" I eyed him out the eye that was halfway open.

"Nothing, but you have to leave her alone."

"You keep saying that, but it ain't easy...," I paused. "We're married," I whispered.

It was like the room got so quiet that you could hear a pin drop on our thick ass carpet. I was waiting for someone to say something, but they didn't. The doctor dropped my pills on the table, told me to call her if I needed her, and scattered out of the room. I'm sure she did not want to be a part of whatever was about to take place.

"What did you just say? Did you say that you two were married?" my ma asked me.

I nodded my head, and pulled out my ring that I had on my necklace, and reached in my wallet to show them our license. Everybody passed it around and read it. It was deathly silent. I mean, I didn't give a damn what they thought, but I was wanting to hear what they had to say.

"Oh, hell no, you have to get this shit⊠" my dad started.

"Is she worth all this son?" my mom cut my dad off. "If you can look me in my eyes and promise me that she is worth it, I won't say another word about it," my mom said, placing her small hand softly on my bruised face.

"Angela..."

"Zip it, Paxton." She snapped her fingers with her other hand, and he shut right up. "Answer me, Phoenix. Is she worth it? Look at your body. I want to go over there and kill him myself."

"Mom." I stared directly into her eyes. "Kambridge Bailey is worth all of this plus more. I'm ashamed that I can't even give her what she deserves. Ma, she massaged my feet after I had been cutting hair all day. She cooks and cleans. Ask Mayhem, he loves her food. She's the sweetest person I have ever met in my life. She already has a business degree and owns her own store, that's doing really well. She took me out the country and showed me a good time, something that I have never done before, and I think I fell even more in love with her. I didn't mean to fall in love with her. If it wasn't for Dad⊠"

"Son..." he cut me off.

"If it wasn't for your dad, what?" my mom cut him off.

He had slowly moved behind my mom and started slowly shaking his head. I guess he didn't want my mom knowing what he wanted me to do. My mom noticed that I was looking at my dad, and she whipped her head around. He quickly put his head down, and she moved in my view of him as if she could cover up his big body.

"Son, look at me and answer me. If it wasn't … for … your … dad … what?"

"If it wasn't for Dad, I wouldn't have even pursued her. We were just two people who kept running into each other, and Dad thought it would be a good idea to use her to find out where her dad had his gold or some shit like..."

She put her hand up and stopped me from talking. She whipped her head back around towards my dad.

"Paxton Allen Bailey," she called his full name. All our middle names are Allen, and when she called us by our middle names, you knew you were in trouble. I know you are NOT still talking about that fucking gold. You don't need that gold. You have done just fine without it. Now you have opened old wounds, and several people are about to be hurt behind this, including Kambridge. End it, now, Paxton. I don't want to hear shit else about that fucking gold, and another thing, you are going to stop trying to force my baby son into the streets. He doesn't want to be in the streets, and he's not going to be in the streets. Do I make myself clear?" my mom snapped at him.

My dad looked like a little puppy dog who had been scolded, and now had his tail between his legs.

"Hello!" She snapped her little fingers. "Answer my question. Do I make myself clear?" she asked.

"Yes, mama. You make yourself clear," my dad whispered, and glared at us when me and Mayhem started snickering.

"Tell your youngest son that you are going to stop trying to force him to be in the streets, AND he is going to be with Kambridge because he truly wants to, and not because of no fucking gold."

My dad repeated after my mom, and I couldn't help but to smirk at him. This was one of the very few times that my mom has EVER taken up for me like this. Yeah, she told him to stop picking on me, but she ain't never put her foot down like this.

"Since we are all on a Kumbaya moment, I might as well tell y'all this too," I said.

I took a deep breath and let my mom in on what I had been doing to get money. I knew that my dad and brother knew what I had been doing, but neither my mom nor dad knew that I had fucked Tracey, and how Cat had been treating me. After I finished telling the story, it was their turn to take a seat and look at me with their mouths wide open. My mom's face turned red, and she started crying, talking about she felt like she had failed me. My dad rubbed her back, comforting her.

"THIS IS ALL YOUR FAULT!" she shouted at my dad.

"Ma, it's all good. I stopped that shit when I married Kam, but Tracey nor Cat is taking it too well."

"Son, you should have told Kambridge the same night you found out. This is not going to end well. Take it from a woman. It's not too late to tell her," my mom offered her advice.

"I don't know when I'll talk to her again. Her dad took everything from her, and she texted me a few hours ago from Kade's phone. She told me that she loved me, and she understood why I said what I said. She also said that her dad has cameras in her house, so she can't even sneak and talk to me. He had her work phone transferred to their house phone. He's literally one step away from handcuffing her in the basement."

"I'mma ask you one last time, Phoenix. IS she worth all of this?"

"Ma, I married her, and I knew how her dad was. So yes, Ma, Kambridge Bailey is worth it," I replied.

"Dad." I looked him in his eyes. "I'm going to kill Kason, if that's the last thing I do, and if I have to die trying," I said to him, and his lips turned upwards.

"That's the best thing that I have ever heard you say," my dad laughed.

For the next few hours, our family laughed and talked like we have never done before. I hated that something like me getting my ass beat, made us come together, but I'd take it. My mom even brought out the baby books, and we reminisced on old times. I finally felt like I was a part of the Bailey family. We strategized how we were going to get my wife to me once and for all, and also how I was going to tell my wife that I had fucked her mom.

After a long ass hot shower, I prayed, popped the pain pills the doctor left for me, and tried to get some sleep, although I knew it was going to be hard since my wife was no longer sleeping next to me. I knew that she was thinking of me, just like I was thinking of her.

I'm coming for you, babe. I promise I'll never let another man take you away from me again, ever, I thought to myself before I fell into a deep sleep.

Kambridge

$\mathcal{E}$ver since that evening my dad dragged me, kicking and screaming away from Phoenix's house, I have been kept under lock and key, not really, but it seems like it. I swear to God my dad might as well keep me locked in the fucking basement in handcuffs. That night I was waiting for my dad to stomp my intestines out my stomach when we got home, but he didn't. He just threw me in my room and slammed the door. He came in hours later, brought me some food, and then told me the new conditions. He took everything from me. He took my regular cell phone, my work phone, my laptop, and even my desktop that was in my room. The only thing that was in my room was my TV, bookshelf, and my bed.

I'm surprised he let me come to work today. He even woke me up for work, and my mom brought me breakfast. I was looking at them both funny. I got dressed and headed to work. When I pulled up and there were two big black men dressed like they were starring for a role for the movie *Men in Black*.

"Can I help you two?" I asked as I approached them.

"We are your security, ma'am. We work for Judge Kason."

I rolled my eyes and opened my door. I was so thankful for Mayhem because he got my store fixed up for me. He saw how I devastated I was after finding out that I had been denied for the loan to get my store repaired. Phoenix wanted to use his money, but I told him no, but I was losing a lot of money with my store being closed. I didn't know who Mayhem hired, but my store looked even better than it did before. He even bought bigger and better machines for me. There was truly no way that I could repay him.

The first internet order came through, and I swear I got it done within two hours because I was so happy to be back at work. I was sitting upfront, flipping through magazines, when Shelly waltzed her ass in the store. I was so happy to see her since I hadn't seen her since before my vacation.

"Hey, girl!" I spoke.

"Girl, what is going on? Who them big ass dudes out there, who barely wanted to let me in the store?" she asked, taking a seat behind the counter next to me.

"Chile, shit has been crazy. Really crazy!"

I filled Shelly in on what happened to my store when I came from vacation, how my dad beat my ass because I found out about the listening device he placed in my suitcase, and how Phoenix had knocked him out because of it. She was shocked when I told her that my dad was trying to charge Phoenix for kidnapping if I didn't end the relationship, and that's how I ended up where we are now.

"So, your parents don't know that you are married to that man?" Shelly whispered.

"Girl, no! Well, my mom knows. She said that Kalena told her, but I don't believe her for one second, especially since Kalena told me that she didn't tell her. I'm assuming she got it from the listening device, but my dad hasn't mentioned it all. He would have probably killed him had I divulged that information. Girl, pull your phone out and call Phoenix for me. I just need to hear his voice," I said to her.

"Girl, I wish I could. They took it when I walked my ass in here. Your daddy is really a bitch. So, I guess it is safe to say that you won't be attending the Playa's Ball tonight?" she asked me.

I gave her a look that told her that she was out of her fucking mind.

"Girl, my dad would kill me. Plus, I don't have anything to wear. You know I have to be the baddest bitch in there."

"BITCH! You have been friends with me all your little life, and you ain't learned a thing or two about me yet. You are going to that fucking ball, and your daddy is not going to find out anything about it. I'm about to be your fairy godmother tonight, hoe! Now, let's take a lunch break and head over to your lil' seamstress," she ordered.

I shut my store down for lunch, and told dumb and dumber that I was going to take a lunch. Do you know these stupid mothafuckas hopped in their truck and followed us? I drove Shelly's car because I ain't know if my dad had my car bugged or some shit. At least they gave Shelly her phone back, so I had her call Shiana Dehreen. She'd been a stylist of mine since I started buying clothes on my own.

"Shiana Dehreen Clothing, how may I help you?"

"Shi, baby, it's me, Kam. How are you doing? Can you do me a big favor?"

"Yes, of course, you know I can. How you been, baby?"

"I could be better. Meet me at the pizzeria, around the corner from my shop, in twenty minutes. Bring me two dress sketches that you can make in like six hours. Make sure you go in the bathroom. I'll explain it to you later," I said, and hung up.

We pulled into the pizzeria, and walked inside. I took a seat near the bathroom, and the Men in Black took a seat at the booth next to us.

"Damn, can I get some privacy?" I sniped at them, but they didn't budge.

We ordered our food, but we didn't talk much to each other because the stupid security guys would hear us, and I didn't want that. I didn't want to give them anything for them to tell my dad. Right on time, I looked up and saw Shiana walking through the door. I turned my head so we didn't make too much eye contact. She walked straight into the bathroom just like I told her to.

"Your majesty, is it okay for my friend and I to go use the restroom?" I stood and curtsied.

One of the guards nodded his head, and stood up to walk us to the bathroom. When I walked in, Shiana was at the mirror, fixing her eyelashes.

"Girl, what the fuck is going on with you, and why I had to meet you in the bathroom?"

"Well, because, … long story short, my dad doesn't want me around this guy⊠"

"Malice," she cut me off.

"Yes, girl, and he took everything electronic from me. So, I haven't talked to him in what feels like years. Shelly says that she has a way to get me to the Playa's Ball tonight, so what can you make me within six or so hours, that is sexy as fuck, and will turn every head tonight?"

Shiana pulled out two sketches. One was a zip down halter top leather dress, and the sides were cut out, being held together by strings. I really like that one.

"You are staring at that one too fucking long. That one is not naked enough. Look at this one," Shelly said, looking at the other sketch.

I looked at the other one, and the first thing I saw was that my whole leg would be out. The WHOLE leg. From my waist, all the way down. All my cleavage would be out, and the top of my shoulders, which immediately made me freeze. Well the dress had sleeves, but the sleeves would be more on my biceps than my shoulder.

"Oh my God! Is this a curtain? What is this?" I asked Shiana. "You know I'm not going to wear my back and stuff out to an event like this," I said.

"This is the dress that's going to have you looking like the black Barbie that you are, at the Playa's Ball. Every head is going to fucking turn when you put this on. Malice's dick is going to bust out of those suit pants, along with the other dudes that's in there. I promise you. We are going to be fly as fuck. I'm going to walk in first because you ain't about to outshine me," she laughed.

I shrugged as Shiana started to pull out her measuring tape.

"I'm still the same size, Shiana," I assured her.

"Girl, please. Look at these hips. That nigga is dicking you down and feeding you right. I love it, but AFTER tonight? Baby, ... he is going to rip this dress off of you," Shiana laughed.

"Girl, he better fucking not, as much as I'm going to pay you for making this last minute for me. Fuck that, but when I think about it, this is nothing by a sexy bath robe," I said. "It'll be worth it, as horny as I am."

Shiana took my measurements, and we left out the bathroom before her. I rubbed my stomach so the men in black wouldn't be suspicious.

"Breakfast didn't agree with me. Sorry," I said.

We took a seat back at our table, and our food was there waiting for us. Moments later, Shiana came out the bathroom and left out the place. Eating in silence was so weird because I had so much to say, but there was no way that I was going to say anything so the men in black could run back and tell my dad.

After we finished eating, we headed back to my store. I called Phoenix from her phone.

"This is Malice," he answered his phone.

"Baby," I whispered and started crying.

"Mama! I miss you so much! Daddy is going to fix this shit, I promise. Do you hear me? Please don't cry. Your husband is going to fix all of this. You know that, right?"

I nodded my head like he could see me.

"Kam, say something," he sighed.

"I'm here," I said.

"You just have to promise me that you won't look at me any different after I handle your dad. I promise you, I'm sleeping that nigga," he snapped.

I didn't say anything. I'm not sure how I feel about him being dead. Phoenix is not a killer; however, I know his dad and brother are. As much as I hated him now, I don't think I wanted him dead.

"Kam, say something," he said.

"I'm just thinking, babe! I just pulled up at my shop and have to get out. If these stupid ass security men see me on the phone, it's probably going to be trouble. I will call you when I can. Please have enough fun for me at the Playa's Ball, tonight."

"Baby, I wish you could come. You won't miss the next one. I love you so much! I don't regret marrying you at all. I promise you I don't. This is going to be a great love story that we can tell our kids. Believe that."

"I love you more, Phoenix," I said, and hung up Shelly's phone.

"Well, girl, I got to get my gown hemmed up, so I will be at your house with your dress and shit, around seven or eight. The ball starts at ten, which gives us more than enough time to have your parents squared away," Shelly said, and got in the driver's side of her car.

The rest of the time at work, I could barely focus because I wanted to know what type of shit Shelly was going to do to get me to go to the Playa's Ball. After finishing my last two internet orders, I boxed them up, and got them ready to be shipped off on Monday. I shut my store down, and got in my car to head home.

The smell of my mom's fried chicken smacked me right in the

face. I went straight to my room and closed the door. Before I could even get out of my clothes good, my parents walked into my room with dinner on a tray.

"Kambridge, I want you to know that I truly apologize for how I treated you the other day, but one day you will understand that I only have your best interest at heart," my dad said.

"I cooked all your favorites. I hope you are hungry," my mom said.

"Nah, I'm actually good. I'll have Kade bring me something when he comes in tonight. Now, if you two don't mind," I said, putting my earbuds into my ears, hoping that they would escort themselves out of my room.

I laid back on the bed and turned my music on in the midst of my mom talking. I don't know what she said, and I don't want to know. She set the tray on the nightstand, and followed my dad out of my room. I sang along to Ruff Endz song "Someone to Love You" until I drifted off to sleep.

Two hours later...

The grabbing of my toe, woke me up in pain. I opened my eyes, snatched my earbuds out, and it was Shelly who was standing at the end of my bed, looking at me crazy.

"Girl, why did you do that?" I asked her.

"I had been calling your name for five minutes, and you didn't hear me."

"Did you think to take at least one of my earbuds out?"

"Whatever, but look, I brought your mom some of my famous rum cupcakes that they love so much. I watched them both eat three a piece," she grinned.

I squinted my eyes at her because she was up to something. She motioned for me to follow her, and I followed her down to the den, and my mom and dad were both laying on the couch knocked out.

"What did you do?" I whispered to her.

"Nothing, just put a few sleeping pills in the cupcakes. They'll be fine in the morning. Not enough to kill them—although I should—but it's enough to keep them knocked out until the wee hours of tomorrow morning," she whispered back. "Now, let's go."

Back in my room, I jumped in the shower and scrubbed with one of my husband's favorite smells, which is my Bobbi Brown, Almost Bare vanilla shower gel. After I got out the shower, I started on my makeup, while Shelly worked on my hair. Since being friends for so long, she has learned to work with my naturally thick hair.

An hour later, we were both staring in the mirror, looking good as fuck. Shelly had on a floor-length strapless gold gown with a split up the side that stopped at the middle of her thigh. Shelly was kind of heavy up top, so her cleavage was on full display and was looking good as hell. She had on a pair of gold Jimmy Choo open-toe shoes. Her hair was pulled up into a bun on top of her head, with a few pieces hanging down on the side of her face.

"Shelly, you look good as fuck! DAMN!" I snapped my fingers.

"Nah, bitch! You are looking fine as fuck. You are going to turn heads," she assured me. "Don't be worried about them fucking scars because you look good as fuck with them. Those are your battle wounds. Trust me. You will have one hell of a story to tell your kids."

I looked in the mirror in this red dress that looked like it could be a curtain liner or something. The dress looked exactly like the sketch that Shiana showed me. I swear this dress was only being held up because of the clear straps that were attached to the half sleeves on the dress. The sleeves only covered from my bicep to my forearm. My cleavage was out, and the split was long, wide, and stopped at my waist. Yes, my waist. So, my wholllllleee leg was out. Thank God for strapless underwear. It fit just like a thong, but no straps, and it stuck to my body like tape. I paired this dress with a pair of nude open-toe Louboutin stilettos, so I was standing tall. It was going to look like this thigh meat had some definition to it, knowing I hadn't worked out a day in my life.

"Come on, girl," Shelly said.

I checked on my mom and dad one more time, and they were knocked the fuck out. Their tongues were damn near hanging out of their mouths like a tired dog. We walked to the front door, and Shelly typed the code in like she lived here.

"How did you know the code?" I eyed her.

"Girl, if you paid attention to when Kade types it in, then you would have it," she said matter-of-factly. I assumed that Kade typed it fast purposely so I wouldn't catch it.

Outside the gate was a black Escalade. The driver had the door opened for us.

"Girl, Uber Premium came through." Shelly laughed as we slid inside the Escalade.

The whole ride across town, I was nervous as hell. I swear I felt as if I was getting ready to lose what little food I had in my stomach. I was wondering what people would say. I kept deep breathing because I didn't want to have an anxiety attack, and the driver had to turn around and take me back home. The driver pulled on a road and started slowing down. I swear when you are on your way somewhere with nerves in your stomach, the damn ride be quick as fuck. When we came to a stop, I looked out the window, and there were expensive ass cars all over the place. There were security guards surrounding the place, so I knew no shit was going to pop off tonight. The driver got out and let us out. Shelly and I walked hand-in-hand to the door. There were two people that were about to open the door for us.

"We are the last two people to walk the red carpet. I'm going in first, and then he's going to call your name. I put Kambridge Bailey on there so the hoes can really be mad," she chuckled.

One of the guards at the door, opened the door for Shelly as soon as the DJ announced her. My heart started beating fast, a mile a minute, because I knew that they were getting ready to call my name. I don't even know what Shelly told them to say, but I couldn't wait.

"You are not your scars, Kambridge LeeAnn Bailey. You are not your scars, Kambridge," I whispered to myself.

"Is there anyone in here who likes chocolate." I could hear the DJ starting to announce me. I hated that he was getting ready to announce me as if I was a stripper. "Last but certainly not least, … we have a beautiful chocolate bar getting ready to walk this red carpet. Her name is on here alone, so if she is as beautiful as she says, then I got first dibs. Come on down the red carpet, Kambridge Bailey." The doors opened, and it was like the room stopped when I got at the top of the carpet. I'm not sure what they were looking at, but a few men's mouths were damn near touching their chest, with their date hitting them, getting their attention. I spotted my brother, who was smirking at me, while entertaining a woman that I was going to ask him about later.

You got this, girl, I thought to myself as I took step by step down the carpet. Scanning the room, my eyes caught exactly who I was looking for: my husband, Phoenix. He was looking at me with his tongue hanging out his mouth.

Malice

I had never seen the final guest list of my dad's Playa's Ball before, but I did look at it this time just to make sure that Cat's name wasn't on it because I ain't want to have to beat her ass. When the DJ called my wife's name, I swear the whole crowd stopped, and everything went in slow motion. My eyes darted from side to side, looking at the men who were looking like they wanted to take my wife home instead of the person that they were with.

Taking in my wife's beauty, I could feel my dick rising in my slacks. My mouth got watery as I thought about how I was going to rip that dress right off her. Don't get me wrong, if I knew my wife was coming, and she was going to wear that shit, I would have told her sexy ass no. But now that I'm among the men looking at her like she just stepped out of a *Playboy* magazine, I was happy that I would be the man that was sliding in her good, wet, and warm pussy. I was happy that she carried my last name and that every nigga in that bitch was going to be jealous as fuck when I walked out with her.

"Damn, who the fuck is that?" Retro asked us, who was standing with me, my dad, Metro, Spice, and Mayhem.

I hadn't introduced her to my friends yet, so they didn't know who she was.

"Whoever she is, she is fine as fuck! Black ass! I bet I can have her ass faced down, ass up at the end of the night. My shit rocking up just thinking about it," Spice replied. "Might even put a few babies in that hoe just for the fuck of it. Damn, I bet her pussy good as fuck." Spice chuckled as he dapped up Retro.

The muscle in my jaw clenched, and I wanted to knock his ass out, but I would give him a pass because he didn't know that she was my wife. In my peripheral, I could see Mayhem raising his eyebrow, but I didn't acknowledge it. My dad was smirking.

"Shit, she is walking this way. Who the fuck she about to say something to? Must be Mayhem," Metro said before taking a sip of his drink. "All the hoes want him."

When she made it close to us, the guys straightened up as if she was getting ready to choose them.

"Mr. Bailey, you clean up nice," she said standing in front of me, wiping a piece of lint off my bowtie.

"Mrs. Bailey, you are so fucking beautiful. Spin around and let daddy see you."

I took her hand and spun her around slowly. My eyes traveled the length of her body, starting with her pedicured white toes, to the top of her thick hair that was pulled up into a ball on the top of her head. She fell into my chest, and I wrapped my arm around her waist.

"Why are your people staring at me like this? Should I have not worn this?" she whispered in my ear.

"They are staring at you because they just said some very inappropriate things about my wife," I said loud enough for them to hear.

I introduced Kam to my homeboys, and I felt like they each held her small hand too long. My dad was the last person that I introduced her to.

"Dad, this is my wife, Kambridge, and Kambridge, this is my dad, Paxton Bailey."

My dad took her hand in his and kissed it, before replying, "Nice to finally meet my son's wife. I've heard so much about you," he said.

"I've heard so much about you too, Mr. Bailey. Beautiful ball you have here. This is my first time ever hearing of this⬚"

"OH MY GODDDD! You are my son's WIFE! Jesus Christ, you are so beautiful. Son, you are SO lucky she chose YOU." My mom rushed by my dad's side, and instantly started gushing over Kam.

I looked at my mom, being dramatic as fuck, and it was funny. She whisked Kam away, and I watched them both until I couldn't see them anymore. It was such an awkward silence once they left.

"Um, my bad, dude, but when the fuck did you get married, and why weren't we invited?" Spice said dapping me up.

"Um, it was kind of a spur of the moment type thing. We got married in St. Maarten almost a month ago," I let them know.

My mom still had Kam doing God knows what with her, so I was bobbing my head to the music, until my eyes caught Cat's ass walking through the crowd toward me with a brown envelope in her hand. I could have sworn I scanned the list several times, and I did not see her name. I heard a loud laugh, and I looked to my left to see my mom and Kam walking through the crowd towards me as well. I felt as if the room was getting smaller, and I suddenly became hot as hell. My eyes kept darting between my mom and Kam, and Cat. Cat took two more steps towards me, and two of my dad's security guards instantly started escorting Cat through the crowd. My heart rate went back to normal almost instantly. I looked around for my dad, spotted him at the top of the stairs, and saw him holding up a glass of liquor, before throwing it to the back of his throat.

Damn, my dad just came through for me in a major way, I thought to myself.

"Baby, your mother is so funny, and I swear I so love her already," she said walking up on me, stumbling a little bit.

"Baby, how many drinks have you had?" I asked her.

"Relax, Phoenix. She has only had two drinks. She's fine," my mom said to me.

"Yeah, Phoenix, I have only had two drinks," she co-signed my mom.

"That's two drinks too many. She doesn't drink like that," I said to her as Kam stumbled again.

My mom went up the stairs to be my dad's side because he was getting ready to give his little speech. The music cut down to a minimum, and everybody stared up at my mom and dad.

"I would like to thank everyone for coming here tonight," my dad said.

Kam grabbed my dick through my slacks, and she grinned.

"Kam, are you tipsy?" I whispered to her.

"So what? You my husband, and I need some dick," she loudly

said and grinned. "My bad. Can I have some dick? I promise, I will be your good little girl, and take it all, with NO complaints," she whispered in my ear.

That perked me up a little bit, making me bite my bottom lip. I put my lips close by her ear, and whispered in her ear while looking around the crowd.

"So, you mean to tell me, I can push your face down, pull your ass up, and give you long and deep strokes, and the *only thing* that you are going to do is throw that ass back on me?"

She latched on to my tux coat, and her eyes closed. I could tell that she was turned on, and the little moan that escaped her mouth gave me more confirmation.

"Kambridge, so you telling me you are going to let a nigga spell his name on your clit, sucking and tugging on it in between each letter, and you are not going to tell daddy to stop?" I whispered, and then bit on her lip.

"Phoenixxx, please," she whispered, leaning her forehead down on my tux.

"Ma, so you are going to let me put this dick in your ass, and you are going to take all of it with no complaints?" I said, and then ran my tongue along the length of her ear.

She crossed her right leg over her left, I'm sure trying to keep the juices from flowing out onto the floor.

"Kam, you're about to cum, ain't you? You better not nut until I can get down there and suck it out. Do you fucking understand me?"

"Mhhhmmm," she groaned. "I need to cum." She looked up at me, and then placed her forehead back on my chest.

"Kam, you like when daddy give you long deep strokes? I loveeee when I got your ass up in the air, throwing that shit back. Watching you cream up my dick, makes me cum fast every time. Do you know what you taste like, ma? Your pussy taste good as fuck, and when your clit is engor...."

"Mhhhmmm." She gripped my coat tighter.

"Kam, if you nut, I'mma slap your ass so hard, five good times, and I'm going to choke you until you damn near pass out while I'm stroking you," I growled in her ear.

"I can't con..."

"Yes, you can!" I assured her.

Just when I was getting ready to talk some more shit, one of her favorite songs came on by Jeremih called "Love Don't Change."

"Let's dance!" she said.

She dragged me out to the dance floor, and placed her arms around my neck. She was so close to me, and this moment felt so perfect.

Girl, I still kiss your head in the morning. Make you breakfast in bed while you're yawning. And I don't do everything, how you want it. But you can't say your mam don't be on it.

She looked up at me as Jeremih sang some of the most relatable words that applied to my life at this very moment.

'Cause I know true love ain't easy. And girl I know it's you because you complete me. And I just don't want you to leave me. Even though I give you reasons.

"Kam." I took a step back to look her directly in her face. "I have to tell you something."

"Shhhh. I don't know when the next time I'll be able to hold you like this, so can it wait? Are you dying or anything that I NEED to know about?"

Yes, I thought to myself because I couldn't bring myself to say the words, so we continued to slow dance until the song was over. Once she started grabbing at my zipper again, I knew we had to get out of there before I got blue balls. I sent my parents and Mayhem a text, letting them know that I was getting ready to get out of there, and they understood.

We were escorted out to Mayhem's truck, and the driver was already waiting for us with the door open. As soon as I got in and shut the door, I pounced on her like the animal I was. The kissing. The touching. All of it was heating my body up like a heater. I ripped that piece of thin material right down the middle, and all my goodies were out.

"Drive," I told the driver as soon as he stepped back in the driver's seat. "We are going to my wife's home, and take your time."

He looked at me and winked before he let the tinted glass window up. Pushing her down on her back, I pressed her legs wide open, and saw the very thin piece of material covering up her pussy. It was already coming off because her juices were saturating it, making it peel away from her skin. I pulled the rest of it off, and dove inside of my heaven on earth. I kissed and sucked all over her beautiful thick pussy lips, before dipping my long stiff tongue inside of her, coating it with her creamy juices. I found that spot that she loved, and started spelling my name on it. I tugged on her engorged clit with my lips, and she damn near shot through that window.

"Phoeniixxx," she moaned my name.

"Hmmmmm," I moaned as I motor boated my lips inside of her pussy lips. The smacking sounds made my dick harder.

I went back to that spot, and started tugging and sucking on it, making her grab a hand full of my hair, keeping my tongue in place.

"Fuckk, I needed this! I needed this! I needed this! Ahhh, daddy, I'm getting ready toooo … ahhhh!" She grinded into my mouth.

I could feel her warm juices coating my chin and sliding down my neck, as I kept my tongue on that spot that was making her go crazy.

I took my coat off and threw it in the back. I unbuckled my pants to free this monster that had been trying to come out since Kam had been grabbing at it in the ball. Damn, I ain't think my dick could get this hard, but it was damn near hurting because of how hard it was. If I didn't get inside of my wife within the next two seconds, I was going to have a heart attack or some shit. That wait was short lived because my wife grabbed my dick, and guided me to my happy place.

Pushing my engorged head inside of my wife's pussy, instantly took me to another world. I sat in place momentarily so I wouldn't nut early, although it would have just given me energy.

"Shhit, baby, move!" she ordered.

"Shut the fuck up! You said that you weren't going to say shit. Why the fuck you talking?" I growled.

She pressed her lips together when she realized what was about to happen. I pulled her ass to the edge of the seat, pulled out, and then plunged deeper inside of her, repeating that action several times. I held her thighs apart, and started stroking her the way that I knew she liked. I looked down at my dick, and my wife was creaming my dick up. Every time I pushed inside of her, it poured out of her pussy.

"Fuck! Kam, I'm in love with you!!" I stared down at her. "Look at me! Who's daddy?"

"You … You are daddy. You are daddy! Fuck me! I need you to beat this pussy up. She missed you," she panted.

"You want daddy to beat it up, huh? You gon' take that dick, bae?"

"Yesss, daddy! I'mma take it. I promise, baby. I promise … ahhh! I'mma take it."

"Turn dat ass over then. You better take this dick too."

I pulled out of her and let her turn over. She positioned herself to face towards the back window. Her elbows rested next to the headrest, and her knees were placed perfectly on the seat, which meant that I was going to be able to get on my knees right behind her, and have the perfect leverage to fuck that pussy the way she wanted me to.

I positioned myself perfectly and plunged inside of her. I started pummeling her tight little snatch. The smacking sounds of our skin, along with the smacking sounds of my wife's wet pussy, had me going crazy.

"Daddddy!! YES!!! PLEASE! FUCK ME! HARDER!" Kam screamed out.

I grabbed her hair, yanking her head back, and started beating it up as fast and hard as I could. The car was slowing down, but I wasn't letting up.

"PHOENIXXX!" she screamed.

"What's up, baby? Daddy hitting that shit right? You like that?"

"Yess! I'm taking that dick," she groaned, and started throwing it back on me, and squeezing her muscles on me at the same time, just like I taught her.

"Throw it back! Throw that shit back, bae!" I commanded.

Smack!

I smacked her on her round ass. "Throw it back harder," I ordered.

"Phoenixx! Ahh!"

"Kam!" I growled.

"PHOENIX!!!"

"KAM!! BABY! FUCKKKK!"

We both yelled out as we came together. That fucking nut came from a place I never felt before. I instantly got weak. I fell over in the seat to catch my breath. Kam started whimpering and sniffling.

"Bae." I nudged her. "What's wrong, did I hurt you?" I asked.

She shook her head no, before she turned around and sat next to me.

"Baby, I swear I don't even know where the tears came from. They just came. That dick is powerful. That is a fucking weapon," she chuckled.

I took off my button-down shirt, and gave it to her to put on.

"Wait a minute. I never asked, how did your dad let you come to the ball?" I questioned.

"Shelly drugged them. Gave them sleeping pills, and she said that they won't be up until the morning. Oh shit! Shelly! Let me text her from your phone right quick, and tell her that I'm already home."

I shrugged because I wouldn't mind if she had given them enough to kill them both. I handed her my phone to text Shelly, and two minutes later, it started ringing.

"CJ is calling. You want me to answer?" she asked.

"NO! No, just reject it, and I'll call 'em back," I said, silently praying that Cat didn't call back.

"Okay." She handed me my phone back.

"I'm going to wait here until I see you in your room. Turn the light on and open the curtain and wave at me. Matter of fact. Yo, Camp!" I said, knocking on the glass.

He let the window down and asked what I needed.

"Let me get one of your phones so I can give to my lady, and I'll get you another one."

He handed me one of his phones, I handed it to Kam, and told her to call me once she gets out the shower. I got out the car and opened the door for her. We kissed passionately for what felt like forever, but

I ain't care.

"Goodnight, wife!" I said, and placed a kiss on her forehead.

"Goodnight, hubby," she giggled.

I watched her walk in the gate, and up the driveway to her house. I stood outside the truck for about five minutes until I saw her bedroom light come on. She opened her curtain and waved at me. I could tell that she was smiling from here. I waved back, even though I'm sure she didn't see me.

When I got back in the truck, we headed back towards to the ball to drop my brother's truck off, and so I could get my car to go home. As soon as I comfortably got in my car, my phone rang, and I knew it was my wife. We talked on the phone until I made it home. She was sleep before I could even put the key in the lock of my house.

Kam

Over the past two weeks, my parents still had me on lockdown, but I was still sneaking and talking to my husband every chance I got. While the men in black would be standing in the front, trying to see if Phoenix was going to ride by, Phoenix and I would be behind the shop in his brother's truck, fucking like animals. Things wouldn't have to be this way if my dad would have just left us alone. After him trying to force me to leave Phoenix alone, or he would execute him right before my eyes, I lost all respect for him. A couple of days ago, when he asked me was I ready to testify against Korupt, I just stared at him like he was speaking another language. After meeting his dad that one time, I could feel in my heart that he was a good guy with a troubled past. My mother-in-law told me all about Korupt, and it made me look at him differently. So I knew I wasn't going to testify against him anyway. My dad would have to kill me.

"Both of y'all stupid anyway. I need to keep my phone on me in case my mom calls," Shelly said at the door.

"Shelly, forget about it," I said to her.

She had been arguing with those fools for the last two weeks about them taking her phone, and I don't even know why, especially since they never gave in.

"You got what I asked you for, girl?" I asked her while rubbing my stomach.

Ever since I had gotten back from St. Maarten, I had been having waves of bad headaches and dizzy spells. I never did make a doctor's appointment like I promised my husband, because I thought it had gone away. Last week, the headaches and dizzy spells were coupled with morning sickness, and I already knew what it was. I was pregnant, which made me extremely excited to be bringing a life into the world with my husband.

"Yeah, girl. I got five of them bitches. I really hope you are pregnant!!" she squealed with excitement, while jumping up and down.

"Relax, girl. I know I am. These are just for confirmation, so me and Phoenix can make our first doctor's appointment together."

I was getting ready to go in the back to pee on these sticks, when Fred, the mailman, came in.

"Hey, Kam! I have some certified mail for you to sign for today." Fred smiled at me.

"Thanks, Fred!"

I walked over and signed the papers. I didn't have time to open it; I needed to get to the bathroom before I peed on myself.

"Shelly, open that for me, girl."

I walked in the back to the bathroom, and poured the contents of the bag on the sink. Five different pregnancy tests, and a small cup for me to pee in to dip the shit in. I peed in the cup, set it on the sink, and started dipping the pregnancy tests in the cup. I washed my hands and waited for the test results. I paced the bathroom floor, praying that I was pregnant. After the five minutes were up, I looked at each pregnancy test, and they all told me what I knew. I was pregnant. I squealed to myself, and ran out to tell Shelly.

"Shellllyyyy," I sang her name while she was looking at the computer.

She turned to look at me, and her face was really red. Tears were in her eyes, with one lone tear that had already fallen down her left cheek.

"Kam, baby, I am so sorry," Shelly whispered.

"What are you sorry about?" I said, walking to the computer to see my husband on video fucking another woman. "Wait…" I snatched the mouse from her, and paused it when the woman turned her head towards the camera. My mouth got watery, and I hurled into the trashcan that was right next to me. I wiped my mouth with the back of my hand. Shelly picked up the package and was getting ready to hand them to me.

"There's more," Shelly whispered. "Kam, before you look at these, please, just…"

I cut her off when I snatched the package away from her. I pulled the pictures out of the package and started shuffling through them. White woman after white woman, and him coming out of different hotels. The last picture was what knocked the wind out of me. My knees got weak, and I had to sit down to process what the fuck I was seeing.

"Shelly!" I started crying my eyes out. "Why does this keep happening to me? Why? Nobody loves me."

"That's not true! I love you! I love you! I love you, Kambridge. I

186

promise." Shelly started crying with me.

"Take your car around back and leave it running," I whispered.

"Kam … you need to come with me. You don't need to be driving right now," she reasoned.

"Shelly, take your car around back, NOW!"

She jumped when I shouted, and ran out the front door. I took the CD out the computer and put it back in the case. I put the CD, along with the pictures, in my purse. I walked in the bathroom and gathered the sticks that I was happy about ten minutes ago, and dumped those in my purse as well. Ten minutes later, I heard Shelly beating on the back door. I yanked the door open and brushed past her.

"KAM! PLEASE DON'T...

The rest was inaudible because I shut her car door, and turned the music up as loud as it could go, and burned rubber out of the parking lot. The whole time I was headed to Malice's house—yes, he was back to Malice—I kept racking my brain trying to think were there any signs.

Yes, there were signs.

"Aarrrggghh!" I screamed, punching the steering wheel.

The first time he had to leave our date, and a few other times, his phone alarmed, and he left. The way he got defensive in St. Maarten about the fucking hoe and her fucking pimp! He is THE HOE!

Speaking aloud to myself, I said, "He told me that he didn't know that white bitch. The night he took my virginity, he told me that he didn't know that bitch. He fucked her and more white women … old white women." *Bleh*. I dry heaved at the thought of him fucking them grannies.

"P.M.B. is mine! Phoenix Malice Bailey. That is the shirt that Cat's ass came into my store and had made. She showed up everywhere. My shop. Our first dinner date. The nail shop. I even thought I saw her getting escorted out at the Playa's Ball. The signs were there. All there. You don't see people that many times like that, … coincidentally," I continued to speak out loud to myself. I was so fucking dumb. I couldn't fucking believe this shit.

"I married this fucking prostitute." I gasped like I just had an epiphany. "He was only using me for my money and my pussy. That bitch! That hoe! All that bullshit he was spewing was just lies. He's no better than my dad. God, why would you do this to meeeee!" I wailed.

Both Malice and Mayhem's cars were in the driveway when I pulled up to their house. I sat in the car for a minute, trying to get my thoughts together. My heart was racing, and my brain was moving a mile a minute. I had never been this angry before. I grabbed my purse and got out to get Shelly's bat out the trunk.

Letting myself in the house with the key that he had given me, I walked around, looking for them both. I could hear them in their game room, laughing loud, and shouting obscenities at each other.

"Bitch ass nigga, where the fuck my money at? Never bet against the Warriors, nigga!" Malice shouted at Mayhem.

"Nigga, I'll give you your lil two thousand dollars!" Mayhem shouted back.

Stepping closer to the door, the light came on in the hallway. Fucking motion light ass house. I couldn't have waited even if I wanted to. Didn't even have time to get my thoughts together before I burst into the room.

"Baby, what you doing⊠" Malice started.

"I want to watch a movie," I said, pressing the ejection button on the game, not giving a fuck about their game. I grabbed the DVD out my purse and popped it in the game.

"Why you got that bat?" Malice asked me, but I completely ignored him.

"You ain't even let me save the game, sis. You better be glad you my bro's wife." He laughed, but this wasn't a laughing matter.

"Stick," I said curtly with my hand out.

The adrenaline through my body was so outrageous to the point where I was fumbling with the stick. I pressed play, and the DVD started playing. Malice and Mayhem both looked like they had just seen ghosts, as I expected them to look. I pointed the bat at the TV screen.

"Malice, who is that?" I asked calmly.

"Kam, please let me⊠"

Pointing the bat at him, and then back at the screen, "Malice, I asked you a fucking question," I asked him calmly once again, but I was getting antsy, and I had to get this adrenaline out my body.

"Baby, it's me, but it's not what it looks like. … Listen, please," he pleaded with his hands up, and eased up from the couch.

I reared back with the bat, and took a swing like I was Sammy Sosa's daughter, and swung at the TV.

CRACKK!

The whole screen cracked with the first swing.

"MALICE! YOU TOLD ME YOU DIDN'T KNOW THAT FUCKING BITCH!"

SMASH!

Bringing the bat over my head, I brought it down onto the game console. Malice tried to approach me, but I swung the bat at his head. Mayhem tried to grab the bat, but I was too quick, and swung it again, making him jump back.

I reached into my purse, pulled out the pregnancy tests, and threw them all at him. He slowly kneeled down to pick them up.

"HERE I WAS, GETTING READY TO COME OVER HERE TO LET YOU KNOW THAT YOU WERE ABOUT TO BE A DAD, BUT NOOO. YOU A FUCKING PROSTITUTE!" I screamed at the top of my lungs while taking a swing at the other game consoles that were behind the glass cases.

CRASHH!

"Miss Lady. Calm down, please. Give me the bat! Don't swing it again!" Mayhem said, easing towards me.

CRASHH!

I swung at the projector that we used to watch movies on, and knocked it on the floor, breaking it into pieces.

"OH, BUT THAT'S NOT ALL!"

I reached into my purse and grabbed the photos that were burning a hole into my purse. I threw them, hitting him square in his chest before falling onto the floor.

"Kambridge, please calm down and listen to me," Malice said.

The tears that were building up in his eyes meant absolutely nothing to me. Nothing. I pointed the bat at the pictures.

"Pick them up and look at them. NOW!" I screamed.

"Kambridge," he whispered.

CRASHH!

I smacked the other case of game consoles, sending it crashing to the ground.

"Look at the fucking pictures, bitch!"

He continued to stare at me, and shook his head slowly. I backed up, and opened the drawer where I knew he kept one of his guns, and pointed it at him. I didn't know anything about using guns, but he needed to get scared.

"Malice … pick … the … pictures … up … and … look … at … them … now!" I spoke through gritted teeth.

He slowly picked the pictures up and looked at them. When he got to the last picture, he dropped them, and looked up at me with a devastated look on his face.

"Kam, please, let me explain."

Holding the gun on them while I walked slowly to the door, I dropped the gun and ran out of the room and went into the kitchen. I could hear their footsteps behind me. I went full Super Saiyan with the bat, and everything with glass, I busted it up with the bat.

CRASH!!

CRASH!

CRASH!

"I TRUSTED YOU! I TRUSTED YOU! YOU FUCKING PROSTITUTE. I BEEN FUCKING A PROSTITUTE!" I screamed as I continued to fuck shit up. "MY DAD WAS FUCKING RIGHT ABOUT YOU! YOU DIRTY DICK BITCH!"

I ran out the front door and started turning Malice's car into a batting cage. Malice and Mayhem both tried to run up on me, but I started swinging the bat wildly at them both.

"DON'T YOU COME NEAR ME!"

As the adrenaline was leaving my body, I was started to cry uncontrollably, while the bat swings on the car got slower, but I wasn't trying to let up. I needed one thing that he cared about to look like how I felt inside: broken.

Mayhem eased towards me. Malice was right behind him, and I picked the bat up, getting ready to swing at them.

"Malice, stay back!" Mayhem ordered. "Miss lady, calm down, and give me the bat. Let's go inside and talk. Just me and you," he said easing towards me.

"He fucked my mom, Mayhem." My voice squeaked from being hoarse. "My mom. He was fucking me and my mom at the same time," I said, and started wailing.

"I know, Miss Lady. Let's go talk about it, okay," he said, continuing to ease towards me. "Calm down, you're carrying my lil' niece or nephew."

"That's the reason why she wanted me to break up with him," I said more to myself than anything. "I married a guy who has been fucking my mom." I chuckled, and then fell to my knees and started crying hard as hell.

"Kambridge, let's go inside and talk about it," Mayhem said, picking me up off the ground.

I snatched away from Mayhem, and reached into my purse, pulling out the stack of money that I was supposed to put in the bank today. I walked over to my husband and started making it rain on him.

"How much I owe you, hoe? How much I owe you for your services, huh?" I asked as I threw the money up in the air over his head.

The muscles in his jawline were clenching. He had his whole bottom lip pulled into his mouth. He was damn near chewing on it. He didn't even have to blink, the tears just started rolling down his eyes, but I ain't care. He needed to hurt. This same man stuck his dick in my mom. He ain't have no right to be mad. His body was shaking, but I wasn't done yet. I picked up the money off the ground and started making it rain on him again.

"How much do I owe you? I was so stupid. That's why you were so comfortable calling my mom Tracey, huh? You remember, back at the store when it first got vandalized. Yeah, I know you remember. The unexplained two hundred thousand dollars that was in your account. I chalked it up to you having a rich dad and a rich brother," I whispered to him. "Matter of fact, Susan was on one of them photos, tsk," I said, shaking my head. "You really fucked me over."

He didn't say anything, but just stared at me with puppy dog eyes full of tears that I ain't give a shit about. I pulled out my wallet and got my credit card out.

"Do you take credit?" I asked. "How much do I owe you? How much are you worth? How much did my mom pay you for that that dick, huh?"

He didn't say anything, but continued to stare at me.

"Kambridge, get away from me." His voice was shaky. "Before I do something I regret."

"I just want to know how much you … wait, get away from you?" I snapped. "Get away from YOU! You fucked my mom, the banker, and God knows who, but get away from you?" I chuckled. "I just wanted to know how much I owed you, but never mind."

I started walking away, but not before snatching my wedding ring from around my neck and throwing it at him.

"Just so you know, I want a divorce."

"No. No, we are not getting a divorce," he said before I got in the car and backed away, leaving him and his brother standing there.

My heart was completely broken, and I swear this hurt more than anything in the world. It hurt more than my dad stomping me out. I wondered if he knew my mom paid for sex. My heart was hurting, and I didn't want to be here anymore. I found myself in front of a gun shop, and I wandered inside.

"Hey, can I help you?" the guy behind the counter asked. His name tag read Ron.

"I want to buy a gun. A gun that I can walk out of here with today," I replied to him.

"Um, rough day? You kind of look familiar."

"Ron, I don't want to chat about my day. I want to buy a gun that I can walk out of here with today. Please, just let me buy a gun," I said, my eyes welled up with tears.

"Sit right here, and let me run a background check on you," he said.

I got frustrated, and rushed out of the store with Ron calling behind me. Zig zagging through traffic, I turned into my driveway in record time. After walking in my house, I ran straight to my room. I knew I could do this, and get away with it, because my bitch ass parents were at work, and Kalena was at school. I pulled out a piece of paper. With tears in my eyes, I started to write …

After scribbling for thirty minutes, I found the sleeping pills on my desk that I had been taking to get some rest at night. I couldn't take this world anymore. I have tried my best to be a good person all my life, despite the way people treated me, but always got shitted on in the end. I was tired. Defeated. Exhausted. The devil and the world had won. I was over it.

God, please forgive me and welcome me with open arms. You know my heart, but I just couldn't take it on this cruel earth anymore. Even the strongest get weak some time.

I shoved the rest of the pills down my throat, and took three big gulps of the water, and laid back on the bed waiting for my life to be done forever.

Kade

*M*y seat was laid back, and this bad broad I met at the Playa's Ball was giving me some of the best top I ever had in my life. She raised up and stared at me with an attitude.

"Your phone keeps fucking ringing. I thought you said you ain't had no hoes," she said.

"Lency … I swear, I ain't got no hoes. I don't know why my phone keeps ringing. My boss knows I'm with you," I said, pulling my phone out my pocket.

I looked at my phone, and I had ten missed calls from Shelly, and ten missed calls from a number that I didn't know. I didn't have any voicemails, so I ran the number through a system, and it came back to a gun shop.

"Watch out, Lency," I said to her.

I pulled up my pants and stepped out the car to call the gun shop back. I thought that Mayhem had stopped through there or something.

"Yeah, this is Kade Lewis. Accountant for Mayhem," I said.

"Uh, Kade, this Ron. I know I'm the last person you want to hear from, but it's important. If I remember correctly, your sister is really dark skinned, with really big hair?" he asked.

"The fuck are you asking about my sister for, nigga? She married," I let him know right off the bat.

"Nah, it ain't nothing like that, but I think you need to go check on her. She came in here a few minutes ago, wanting to buy a gun. She looked distraught. I tried to call you while she was here, but she ran out before I could put the phone to my ear. Check on her, man," he said and hung up the phone.

My heart instantly started racing because Kam had never shot a gun in her life, yet alone saw one, until she got with her husband. I jumped back in the car and told Lency that I had to take her to Starbucks up the street, and call her an Uber because I needed to get home quick.

"Don't be like that. My sister is my heart, and I need to go check on her. You can't come to my house yet, ma! Don't be mad. I'll make it up to you," I said to her when I pulled up to the Starbucks.

I pecked her on her pouty lips, and unlocked the door for her to get out. As soon as she was safe inside of the Starbucks, I dialed the house phone, and it rang twenty times, and no one answered. I weaved in and out of traffic, trying to make it home. Sitting at a red light, I started getting anxious. Gripping the steering wheel as if I was getting ready to take off like a Nascar Driver, I burned rubber as soon as the light turned green.

I made it to the house, rushed into Kam's room, and screamed like a little bitch. My sister was shaking violently, and foaming at the mouth.

"Kam, baby, what did you do?" I cried, rushing to her side.

TO BE CONTINUED

Looking for a publishing home?

Royalty Publishing House, Where the Royals reside, is accepting submissions for writers in the urban fiction genre. If you're interested, submit the first 3-4 chapters with your synopsis to submissions@royaltypublishinghouse.com.

Check out our website for more information: www.royaltypublishinghouse.com.

Text ROYALTY to 42828 to join our mailing list!

To submit a manuscript for our review, email us at
submissions@royaltypublishinghouse.com

Text RPHCHRISTIAN to 22828 for our
CHRISTIAN ROMANCE novels!

Text RPHROMANCE to 22828 for our
INTERRACIAL ROMANCE novels!

Get LiT!

Download the LiT eReader app today and enjoy exclusive content, free books, and more

Do You Like CELEBRITY GOSSIP?

Check Out QUEEN DYNASTY!
Visit Our Site: www.thequeendynasty.com